# DEATH-LINK

# DEATH-LINK INK

Copyright © *2017 Paul Shirk*

Paul Shirk Author/Speakers Agency can send authors to your live event. For more information or to book Paul Shirk at an event contact:

Printed in the United States of America

ISBN 978-1-945384-24-0

# DEATH-LINK

*Paul Shirk*

**For Kim**

**Thank you for your love and endless support.**

# PROLOGUE

The road is getting steeper as my body accelerates to the point of losing control. *Maintain, Ken, maintain... Damn, she's beautiful.*

Trees line the curve, canopying in a perfect arc. *Life is good.* Lucy disappears from sight once more, showing me dominance. All it does is turn me on. She is the love of my life; the melody to my song. *I wish I had half her energy*, I thought. *How does she do it?* Sweat pouring off my face, I yell "Bitch" in a playful tone and duck under the Jacobson's arbor. *She won't know what hit her.* Olivia, the Jacobson's dog, is barking, giving away my position. This just makes Ms. Lucy Grey giggle and push it into overdrive. She's on to my game. Breaking the curve, purple irises are flying; I catch a glimpse of perfect buttocks as she shuts the rear sliding glass door behind her.

"Aha," she says. "That's for the 'bitch' comment."

As I watch that infectious smile and hear the latch flip, I know she is heading straight for the front door.

Doubled over, hands on my knees, I can feel my heart pounding. It tells me that I'm alive. I code the garage and go right for the Makita. Standing at the slider again I can see Lucy's shiny blue eyes inches from my face, peeking over the rim of a sweating glass of ice water. *I still can't believe how she makes me feel.* I cannot bear the thought of a life without her.

Raising the cordless drill to my shoulder, I shake my head and grin. "I built this house; you don't think I could take it apart?" I say with a raise of my eyebrows.

A pause, a wink. She flips the lock, leans in seductively, gives my lips a lick and heads for the shower. *I love you.* Life is good… for now.

I wipe my head with a towel and sit at my desk cooling off a bit, giving Lucy a moment alone in the shower; just a moment, though. Lights blinking, my eyes go to my phone without my head moving. *Back to reality.*

The first message is from Lucy's mother: "Birthday is coming up. What are you doing for her?" *Got to love her.*

The second message is reminding me of my root canal appointment on Monday. *Shoot me now.*

The third is a charm. The call I've been waiting for. It's my long-time friend, business associate, partner in crime -- or should I say partners, plural. Because wherever Don is, John is. Twins. Night and day.

"Hey, Ken. It's Don and John." Their message always starts that way, but brings a shake of the head and a smile. If it was any different it wouldn't be right.

"Hey, dipshit. We got it," John chimes in.

I know exactly what he means. You're probably thinking a business deal, but no. This is all pleasure.

"Just call us when you get done playing with your Barbie," Don finished.

"I still don't know what she sees in you. She must have grown up at the ballpark eating peanuts. Tell her to call me if she wants a real man to come on over. Later, fag." John laughed and hung up. *You've gotta love them.*

I picked up the phone to return Hanz and Franz's call. Then I thought, *nah, not yet. My queen awaits.*

# Chapter One

On the northern California coastline, set back in the woods among the coastal redwoods -- home of the world's tallest trees -- was Dillon Maxwell's private estate. Once a beautiful structure with well-manicured grounds, a billiards room, two swimming pools, tennis courts, and a kitchen equipped to feed the United States Navy; now, this 10,000 square foot shell was just one of Dillon's so-called hideouts. If you had half a brain and at least one good eye, you could tell who occupied this once beautiful estate. This was not a very stealthy group.

Dillon was entertaining in the master suite. She was a 19year-old southern belle they had picked up in Houston late the night before. Smooth skin, Marilyn Monroe hair and an hourglass figure. She was stripped to her birthday suit and secured to the cold marble wall with eye bolts and metal ratchet restraints. Her flesh shivered, raising goose bumps and hardening her nipples as Dillon brushed his coarse face against her body. Drawing in a long, audible sniff, he inhaled her scent of light vanilla and exhilarating youth.

The sounds coming from the room were submissive with a clear tone of fear. Eight of Dillon's men filled the great room. They were heavily armed and wondering how long this was going to take. Some expressed their opinions.

"I don't want to hear another word," said Jax as he shattered a bottle into the stone fireplace. "What do you think you guys get paid for? Keep your opinions to yourself."

"All I'm saying is this shit is getting old," said John Boy, standing up in protest.

A .50 caliber round cracked through the front window and tore through his shoulder. His arm dismembered and struck Ray in the face with such force that it broke his nose.

"Holy fuck! Hit the ground!," Jax bellowed.

The second round took John Boy out for good; the bullet struck him in the chest and exited through his back, showering the wall with blood and heart matter, and leaving a hole in his back the size of a large Skippy jar. By the time John Boy's limp, lifeless body hit the floor, the others were in a covered position, guns drawn and minds in combat mode. This was not their first rodeo. "Tommy, do you have sight?" Jax asked. "How many are there?"

"Two… No, three… We've got three birds, no ground. Two are flanking the sides."

"We have to get to the Hauler, now. It's the only way to bring 'em down," Sands yelled.

"Give me some cover," shouted one of the men from the back.

A thick cloud of black dust came billowing through the front of the house, shattering the windows as a 20-foot-long combat-equipped hovercraft descended sideways to a stop, guns blazing.

The weapon Dillon had just obtained was located in the Hauler and was potentially his future: a launcher of encapsulated energy. When fired at velocity, upon impact it would reverse the electrical charge in a hovercraft, causing the magnetic field to fail and, in turn, bring down the beast. Dillon's brain was spinning. As his men were under fire, all he could think of was his new toy. Now he would be able to test it out in a live situation.

"Don't worry, honey bee, I'll be back in a few," Dillon told his prize, his voice gravelly.

He pulled his scarred leather boots over his tattered wool socks, racked his sawed-off shotgun and bolted through the door like a bull in a china shop. Dillon got to the Hauler within minutes. Located on the top floor was approximately 2,000 square feet of a garage area with a two-ton retractable steel roof system. The roof closed to the center, and when opening could clear a spot large enough for the Hauler within seconds, despite its bulk.

The vehicle was a large box. Thirty-six feet in length, modeled from the old Airstream travel trailers. Bench seats ran down the center with expanded metal lockers lining the walls. A sleeper compartment was located behind the cab with a small kitchenette. The Hauler was equipped with weapons, ammo, food, clothing, and oxygen tanks. The back doors opened out, and the front windshield hinged upward for driver access. Long runs or high altitude runs were typically auto-navigated with GPS, and the vehicle could move in excess of 200 miles per hour fully loaded.

These hovercraft vehicles basically functioned the same no matter how big or small. They respond to the Earth's own magnetic field using a mathematical influence of electrical currents. By speeding up or slowing down electrical charges, the vehicle would rise or fall from the Earth's opposing magnetic pole. Angling would provide movement forward or backwards. The faster the current, the higher the rise; which also created a stronger magnetic field around the body of the craft, virtually rendering it bulletproof and near impossible to impact with other fields. This is where the launcher came into play.

Sure that an ambush lay await above, Dillon did not even consider retracting the roof. He would be a sitting duck. He quickly pulled on a vest loaded with various types of grenades, filled the empty pouches with 10 encapsulated energy rounds and strapped his new 80-pound precision launcher to his broad back.

Dillon swung around and held his Remington in the face of two of his men. With cold, steel-gray eyes, and a large vein protruding from his forehead, he stared through the men as he lowered his weapon to his side. Tossing one of them an M3 tripod for the launcher, he gave calm, but firm orders.

"You, follow me," he said, looking directly at one of the men. "And you, activate communication and assemble the men at the east side, second floor and spread 'em out. Be ready. We're going to bring these fuckers down."

# Chapter Two

      Don and John hit the Hearts 24-Hour Fitness close to Ken's place. Don was old-school and liked to stay fit by lifting iron; John went with it. Most people used Virtual Reality Relaxation Therapy to shape their bodies and improve brain function -- also known as a "mind gym." This process was originally developed for professional athletes. It was proven to guide them to excellence and provide a drive to succeed in life. Not only did they learn at a faster rate and gain more clarity of thought, they were also able to send their muscles through a series of contractions, improving muscle mass and flexibility in joints. Don was skeptical of the whole process. Plus, he liked sweating, putting the time in, and feeling the burn.

"We can start out by incorporating 20-minute sessions with our workout, you know?" said John as they walked through the automatic doors.

The Hearts facility was enormous: three stories of panoramic glass fronts, exposed I-beams, tension cables, and come-alongs for shearing the structure. State-of-the-art would be an understatement. Old-school meets new-school. It provided all aspects of the classics: cable machines, free weights, aquatics, aerobics, cardio, swimming, tennis, racquetball, you name it. Plus the modern mind gym, extensive spa treatments, oxygen bars, vitamin drips, and rejuvenating baths. Professional staff and top notch security had put them on the cover of Forbes more than once.

"Good morning, boys. Hi, John," the 22-year-old eye-candy receptionist said with a wink.

John responded with a wink of his own and pep in his step, "Well, hello Stacy."

"She doesn't like me, huh?" said Don as they glanced up at the security recognition screen.

"Maybe it's because you won't book a session," John shot back.

"Would you stop with the mind gym crap? They fucked with our brains enough when we were kids."

"Stacy said she learned Spanish in three sessions and toned her abs at the same time."

"Then go play with Stacy. Maybe you two can frolic in the virtual flowers and hold hands," Don said with sarcasm.

"You're an ass. Let's hit the bench. See if you can keep up this time."

They made a brief stop in the locker room and both went to their favorite lockers to unload and secure their personals -- creatures of habit. Don wasted no time and headed straight to the elevator. John followed suit, one step behind.

"If Ken doesn't call by the time we're done, we should pay him a visit," Don said, briefly looking over his shoulder.

John nodded in agreement, biting his lip, still a little miffed at his brother.

With no verbal response, silence assaulted the elevator and Don felt his emotions waver. They exited the ride and quickly moved to the bench bar in the corner with a view of the Pacific.

"Get over it. You're dragging me down," Don said with an irritated look on his face as he loaded a 45-pound plate to the bar. John just shook his head and tried to clear his thoughts so Don could not feel his frustration. Twins connect in many ways. They share identical neural pathways and this creates a natural bond between them. Some say it is so strong they will share death: they were brought in together, they will leave together. Don and John showed many traits of connection. Sharing physical pain or actual injuries of one another was low on the charts. Their bond was more emotional, sharing highs and lows, stimulation or depression. They communicated very well, as if the other's thoughts invaded their own.

As Don and John were growing up they struggled for individuality, while others looked to harness this connection. During their upbringing they were used as test babies, poked and prodded from infancy to adulthood. Their parents made a small fortune at their expense. Allowing them to not only be observed, but to be forced into situations creating pain, fear, stress, joy, and depression just to monitor brain activity. They were separated for long lengths of time and then brought back together. Their dreams were studied and analyzed. Nothing was sacred.

Following the study of Don and John and numerous other sets of twins over the past century, the powers-that-be had created a bonding procedure to link two people -- who have individual neural pathways -- to each other. By shocking the pathways simultaneously into the same sequence, they can share a twin-like connection. As well as sharing emotions and dreams, they may experience a type of telepathic communication with one another. This bringing two people as close as possible, over two million had made the connection... and still counting. This procedure was called Neuralinking and only took about half an hour of semi-discomfort and a brief precautionary recovery time.

Hearts was slotted for a Neuralink facility in the near future. Some of the headlines had stated they may be due for a name change and suggested "Hearts and Brains Fitness Center" as a punch line.

"You're still thinking about it?" said Don. "You can't escape me."

"I... can't... help it," John said as he pushed through 425 pounds of iron, forcing air out through his pursed lips. "I just want you to be open-minded about it -- no pun intended."

"Okay, you win. We can give it a shot if it will make you feel better... wait a second. Did you just manipulate me?" Don said with a scowl on his face. "I'm supposed to be the strong one."

"If you're the strong one, show me. Four reps, 445 pounds, and don't ask for help this time. Don't even think about it, chump." John's mood changed on a dime.

"This mind gym better not make me touch myself. I've heard stories."

"You should be so lucky." John laughed. "You want to hit on some tail at the gun range later? It's ladies' night."

"Sounds good to me, let's see if Ken wants to join us. Just don't tell Lucy about it being ladies' night." Don smirked.

\*\*\*\*\*

Lucy and I were enjoying the afternoon together after an invigorating shower experience. We both had a vodka-and cranberry in hand and were basking in what little sun the haze let through over the gray Pacific. We had a small view of the Santa

Monica Pier from the ocean side porch of my home: an early California bungalow style, with thick, tapered pillars of rock on either side of a beautiful mosaic four-tread staircase, opening to the white sands of a nearly forgotten Pacific front.

Lucy put her drink down and was focusing her old Nikon once again. Photography was not only her passion, it was her career. She had sold numerous photos to all the major magazine and advertising agencies. Several billboards across the country displayed her work, as well as some overseas. Black and white contrast shots were her forte. She had an eye and a technique that was unrivaled.

The first time I came into contact with Lucy, she was behind a lens. She was shooting a wedding for a friend of my fiancé. Six months later we hired her for our own wedding. I could not take my mind off of her. Her unshakable confidence, stunning figure, long blonde hair, and a mesmerizing toothy smile had burned in my mind. At our rehearsal dinner, Lucy came clad with her camera around a slender neck, tight denim jeans with a bright fitted red blouse and red stilettos. One look at her and I knew what had to be done. Call off the wedding and re-evaluate my life. I paid Lucy for her time, and with youthful butterflies in my stomach, I asked her to have a drink with me. Now, three years later, here she was again, lens zoomed out to the pier and I still couldn't take my eyes off of her.

"What do you think about Neuralinking?" I said, slightly under my breath.

"Don't tease me, Ken," she replied.

"I'm not kidding. We could do it on our way to Vegas."

"We're going to the Expo?" she said as she dropped her camera to her lap, turned and looked directly into my eyes for confirmation.

"It's a go. Don called earlier and said we got in."

"This is going to be awesome," she said, pulling her knees to her chest like a giddy child. "Ken?"

"Yes, my love?"

"Are you serious about Neuralinking?" She had a look about her when she said this -- a look that told me not to fuck with her emotions.

"Very," I replied in a clear tone, holding her gaze.

Just as the words left my lips, two soft tail gliders came whipping down over the house to a halt at the foot of the porch, stirring up sand and flinging dirt. I reached to my side and raised my sawed-off double-ought to a combat position as the dust cleared.

"Assholes! Don't you guys know how to use a phone?" I yelled.

"Hey, fuck stick. Where is your phone?" John said in a mimicking tone as he glanced at Ken, flipping the guard on his helmet and disconnecting the oxygen lines.

"Good point."

They shut down the gliders and eased them down on a smooth patch of sand.

"I hate it when you do that," said Lucy. "Why can't you use the pad? Ken's home vac clogs up at least once a week. We don't need you guys adding to it. I can't even see the sun, for Christ's sake."

Don jumped over the handrail and took the last two steps like a flash of lightning. "Give me a hug," he said as he draped his black duster over a chair and had his arms around Lucy before she could flinch.

She laid her head into his massive chest and gave a little whimper of love. Lucy could definitely take care of herself, but to a man like Don, well, let's just say she was glad he was in her corner. She gave his stomach a mercy tap for release and headed to meet John with a hug as well.

I'm good with a fist bump from each of them. Their size intimidates me, always has. "You guys are going to be jealous," I said. "I'm going to grab some beers. Meet me on the pad." I disappeared into the house and Don and John looked to Lucy for clarification. All they got was a shrug and a grin.

I grabbed some cold porters from the fridge and headed through the house to the garage in front. The door rose as I saw their feet and then their heads about knee high as they peeked under the rising door in anticipation. Popping the tops on the beers, I handed them out like a proud new father with a fist full of 'it's a boy' cigars.

"What do you think?" I said, just a little too smug.

"Holy crap. You fucking trust fund babies make me sick," said Don. He ignored his beer and circled my new glider. John's look was wide-eyed, like sanity had left the building. He had a slight tick in his face and gradually exaggerated it. "Code me in. I have to ride this now."

"Like hell," I said. "I might be dumb, but I'm not plumb dumb."

"What did it set you back, bro?"

"Well, bro." I smirked back. "Put it this way: I had to up my life insurance policy. I wouldn't want to be a financial burden to anyone."

Don made a pfft sound. "Whatever, I could pay off my house with this thing."

"How fast does she go?" asked Don.

"Two hundred eighty miles per hour up in the jet stream. She won't go much higher, but she is practically bulletproof at that altitude. All-leather interior and both seats recline. You could sleep in this thing. It has an aquatic mode, manual mode, and full GPS auto mode. You name the mode and she's got it."

"Man, that paint job is sick. You had Carlos do that, huh? It's got his name written all over it," John said as he caressed his hand down the side of the glider.

"Hey, let's cruise down to Mission and have a drink at Ale's. We can talk about the Expo. I need to put some miles on this puppy anyway," I said as I downed my tasty beverage and removed the center back support from my new Batmobile -- that's what Lucy called it. That way she could lean back into my chest for the ride.

We came down hard over the roofline of the house, hitting the foamy water where the tide was thin. We had just enough angle to put some salt water on Don and John, paying them back for the sand attack back at the house. Hovering about forty feet from the shoreline and about ten feet from the surface of the vast ocean, we set a course for the Ale House. Briefly toggling to manual mode, we made a quick circle around the pier for a photo op that Lucy couldn't pass up. She angled her camera and took some incredible shots of the pier, surfers, and houses that melded into the side of the mountain. I spotted Hanz and Franz creating squiggly lines in the water like two children in a huge bathtub with their plastic toy Sea-Doos that grandma gave them.

"Kids," I said, rolling my eyes at Don and John.

"So, you really want to do this," Lucy whispered.

"Do what?" I replied with a grin on my face.

"Don't be an ass."

"Of course. I've been thinking about this for a long time now, and I really want to have it done before the Expo. It's going to be so cool."

Lucy turned her head back and kissed me. "Did you tell Don and John?"

"No, and I don't think we should."

"My thoughts exactly. They'll just try to talk us out of it."

"See, we are practically linked already." I gave her a tight squeeze, not wanting to let her go.

"Great minds think alike."

# Chapter Three

Bullets riddled the house with precision as the two crafts in the rear of the estate opened fire on the corner, creating an X pattern of molten slugs. The one in the front continued to fire straight through to the forest behind the sprawling estate. This was not the first time Dillon had been targeted, and would definitely not be the last. He was a nasty man who knew right from wrong, but the pleasure was too great in the latter. Drugs, firearms, automobiles, prostitution, and gambling. If there was a dollar to be made or extorted, Dillon would jump in swimming and leave the rest in his wake. He did not care who was outside firing upon him, or why. All he cared about was that every last one of them would soon cease to breathe.

Glass, wood, drywall, and siding fragments exploded through the house. Structural damage was imminent. Dillon motioned for the tripod with his hands. He sighted one of the crafts through a 10-lite wood French door. It was hovering over an empty lap pool with overgrown ivy cascading over the edge to a swampy bottom filled with old slimy lawn furniture.

*Perfect,* he thought. *Hope you like frog's legs.*

With an eerie calm he assembled the tripod and mounted the launcher. Loading a round and adjusting the sight, he felt his adrenaline spike to a new level. *If this works, we're in the money.*

He gave the command to return fire, knowing he could lose men. Dillon positioned the muzzle in the bottom corner pane of the door and took the shot. With the sound and flash of a rocket launcher he gave away his position. He instantly rolled to his back, planted his feet on the wall and pushed off, sliding across the tile. Bullets ripped through the door, blowing it off its hinges.

"Direct hit," confirmed his look-out.

The sound of the craft's composite body connecting with the plaster of the pool was unmistakable. The assailant's crew was disoriented, ears bleeding from the concussion of the impact and scrambling in a state of panic. Two Mac-10s opened fire from the house, relentlessly demolishing the hovercraft in its vulnerability, confining it to a grave of plaster and muck. A thousand 9 mm rounds per minute ripped through the bodies of the crew, completing the crime scene with crimson death.

Dillon quickly got to a vantage point and reloaded the launcher. The pilots of the remaining mercenary crews realized they were seconds from destruction and raised their elevation in retreat.

Dillon was in the perfect position to test distance and accuracy. He exhaled slowly through his nostrils, placed the crosshairs and gently squeezed the pad with his finger. With a dead-on strike the hovercraft jolted, descending uncontrollably. Dillon watched as it impacted a huge redwood thirty feet off the ground, creating a vaporizing explosion.

The last shot was going to test not only the weapon, but his capabilities as well. He adjusted the scope, took a calm breath and reloaded. The craft was accelerating fast, up and away above the forest. It was the size of a softball before Dillon locked on the sight and pulled the trigger. Seeing the explosion on the horizon confirmed impact. Dillon closed his eyes and saw dollar signs.

"Jax... you there?" He spoke into his mic, folding the tripod. He kissed the stalk of the launcher and breathed in the fired scent. "What's the damage?"

"John's dead, boss, and Luke's been hit. He's bleeding out fast, man."

Dillon paused for a moment... But just a moment.

"... Put one in his head," he said. The words came out calloused and full of ice.

Grant was holding Luke in his arms as Dillon's words registered. Luke gasped for air, unable to voice a protest. Grant looked up with a pleading expression, making eye contact with Jax. Jax motioned to move with his head. Grant moved slightly but kept his eyes locked on Jax. Without further hesitation, Jax pulled his Glock and put a 9mm round into Luke's forehead, painting Grant with Luke's blood.

"What the fuck, Jax?"

"Time's wasting, move out."

Jax knew that Dillon would not want to hang around any longer than necessary. He knew the routine and the response time of the authorities.

Many crimes went unnoticed in these lawless times, but the scale of this raid and the explosions in the forest were sure to draw the attention of the local police. It was just a matter of time before Special Forces would be dispatched to cover the scene.

It's not that law enforcement wouldn't put the resources into tracking down a serial killer like Dillon, but most of the manpower and funds went into securing the nation from terrorism. With the skies open, jurisdictions were shattered and border control non-existent. The military relied on cryptologists to track the threat and the SEAL teams to remove it.

Dillon had cravings, and even with his tactics drawing attention he did not want to tangle with the SEALs and expose his game. As long as it was simple drug running or minor arms deals they could co-exist. There were bigger fish to fry.

"Jax... get up here," Dillon spoke with disappointment in his voice.

"10-4."

Jax walked in to the master suite and put a hand on Dillon's shoulder. "I'll take care of it. Why don't you wait upstairs?" he said to his long-time friend.

Dillon's head was hung in sheer depression as he took in the girl's lifeless body. Seeing her this way would have had the opposite effect if it was by his hand that she drew her last breath. Bullets had thrashed her mid-section. Blood spilled from her mouth down her chest, dripping to a large crimson pool on the floor. He took her face in his hands, pulled her chin up, leaned in as he dragged his tongue over her lips; breathing in the aroma of death, iron, and obsession with an oriental perfume of spices, warm and exotic.

"My favorite," he whispered to himself and exited the room, licking his lips.

Grant passed by Dillon in the hall and not a word was exchanged. He was still wiping Luke's blood from his face when he saw the girl.

"You know he's a sick fuck," he said quietly to Jax, knowingly crossing the line, but hoping for an ally.

Jax looked at Grant and did not verbally respond to the comment. He did not need to. Grant got the point and looked to the floor. "Catch," Jax said and tossed a restraint key to Grant. "Wrap her up."

Jax turned and briskly walked out, keying his mic. "Salvage what you can and get to the Hauler."

Tommy retracted the roof and fired up the Hauler while Dillon was securing the launcher, rounds, and riot vests.

Jax climbed in. "That was intense, man." He shook his head to wind down. "I put Ray and Grant on drop duty. They'll meet us at the Sedona shop."

Thousands of bodies dropped from the sky every year. Some deceased, some not. Some, under their own will. Rural areas were an easy target and could go unexplored for ages. The Grand Canyon was littered with bones and infested with flesh hungry vultures. And it just so happened to be in a direct route to Dillon's shop in Sedona.

"Did you see what the launcher did, Jax?" Dillon said. "Unfucking believable."

"We're going to need some inventory before the Expo," Jax said with excitement on his face.

"Hell yeah, tripods too." Dillon's mind was spinning. He shook his finger and pointed toward Jax. "I want swivel mounts for The Claiborne. One on the upper deck, just in front of the captain's cabin and one on the sun deck by the hover pad. Can you make that happen?"

"No problem, Kemosabe. I'll have the mounts put on before we get down there. They already have the specs."

The rest of the crew secured weapons and strapped in for the lift. Within minutes they were airborne and approaching max speed toward Arizona.

Ray and Grant detoured slightly east out over the vastness of the canyon for the drop. Ray's face was throbbing and his nose needed to be reset. The sky was cloudless and a clear blue up high. Even through Ray's watery eyes and Grant's bloodshot anger, they could appreciate the view.

They descended into a haze of sand for camouflage, killed the power to clear the magnetic field from the hovercraft, and dropped the pale, blood-caked corpse of the Marilyn Monroe lookalike. Ray powered up and accelerated the craft with perfect timing and the skill of a veteran. Fourteen years with Dillon had perfected the art of the drop.

# Chapter Four

The Ale House was quite large for a micro-brewery. The entire front was lined with dark tinted glass encased in weathered hickory rubbed with a black creosote stain. I, for one, liked it. A small rusted iron sign labeled the entrance. The atmosphere inside was far different from the western-like beaten exterior. All surfaces were concrete, polished glass smooth, exposing beautiful aggregate beneath thick glaze. The non-glass walls were lined with copper mirrors, and track lighting/fan combinations adorned the ceiling. The booths and bar stools were skinned with rich rustic leather for the long haul.

Lucy and I walked in and asked for our favorite booth in the corner. Ocean shot, TV shot, people shot, and if it's not available we'd take the bar.

"We have two thugs following us," I said to the cute little hostess wearing an Ale House shirt which was two sizes too small for her frame. She had a look of concern and opened her mouth to speak but nothing came out.

"No worries, they're friendly. Send them our way, doll," Lucy said with a wink.

"Four porters in the back, *por favor*," I shouted to the barkeep, holding my hand up with my thumb folded in.

"The boys will have fun with her," Lucy said. "Am I going to know what you're thinking when you look at girls? I hope not."

"I'm not sure if you'll know my thoughts necessarily, but you might feel my excitement… just kidding. Do you want to feel my excitement right now?"

"Stop it," she said, dragging her words. "Yes."

The pub was one of our old faithful's. It always had great food, good, consistent live music and a pleasing, colorful atmosphere. It seemed to be a requirement for the brew staff to be bearded and have a full head of hair curling under the standard Ale House baseball cap. The requirements for the ladies appeared similar to Hooters, but slightly less slutty.

We received our first round of beers and then spotted the Thompson Twins walking toward us. They were rubbernecking the hostess as she smiled and pointed to our table.

"Man, I'd eat a mile of her, you know what? Just to see where it came from," John said, taking his seat, eyes still on the girl.

Don grabbed his beer, half toasted already, and took a substantial gulp, ending it with a satisfying nod.

"Why… Why do you have to be so crude?" Lucy said, dropping her hands to the table in an 'I give up' gesture.

"Why does a dog lick his balls?" he spat back.

Lucy just rolled her eyes and enjoyed her beer.

"A toast, to Vegas." Don said, raising his glass.

"Vegas," we responded simultaneously and touched rims around the table.

"Mmm… that's a good beer," I said.

"Great head," John replied with what he thought was perfect timing.

"Would you just shut up?" his brother scolded. "Have some respect." Which we all knew was not needed. Lucy could be worse than the guys when her mood fit. "So here's what we've got. Two rooms at the Hilton Towers -- with a view, I might add -- four passes for the square, full access, floor seating, and transportation in and out of the city. You don't get any better than that." "Sweet. So what are the dates?" I asked.

"August 16$^{th}$ through the 30$^{th}$ is the Expo. The rooms are comp'd from the 16$^{th}$ through the 23$^{rd}$. After that you couldn't book a room if you tried."

"You guys won't be back from Alaska until the end of August, right?" I asked.

"What do you mean, you guys?" said John. "You're not going?"

"Can't do it this year, boys, you're going to have to count me out."

"We can't cut two weeks off the season and lose a deckhand too," Don squeaked in frustration.

"Why do you have to fish then? Can't you fish any time of the year?" Lucy asked.

"Our contract is only for salmon and halibut. So we have to hit the peak times to make enough dough to live on the rest of the year."

"That means early summer, like May through the end of August," John added.

"I'll pick up the slack for you guys. And don't worry about the expenses at the Expo," I said. "Just let me know what you're short."

"That's not the only problem. We'll struggle making our client's quota," said Don. "Why are you skippin'?"

"I just promised Lucy I would spend the summer with her this year. Plus, that's fucking work up there."

"Sorry, guys." Lucy sheepishly smiled.

"Our cousin has been begging us to take him out anyway. He turns 19 this year and wants to get his feet wet," Don said. "He'll get more than his feet wet, that's for sure. He doesn't know what he's getting into," I said. "Did you know the U.S. Coast Guard dragged more than 200 bodies from those waters last year alone? And guess what?" I whispered. "Some were dead."

"We don't listen to those stats, Ken, makes a man weak," Don said.

"Yeah, and apparently it makes a man want to puss out and spend the summer with his girlfriend, too," John added.

I looked at John and took a drink. "It's not working."

John shrugged his shoulders. "Another round, barkeep," he shouted, raising his empty glass, shaking it in the air with an 'I'm dying of thirst' expression.

"So, tell me about security," I asked Don.

"Security for what?"

"For my $120,000 Bugatti Glider, for instance. You said transportation into the city. I'm not leaving my bike in the desert with some toothless trailer trash."

"The security is 5-Alarm, the same outfit that handled the last three Expos. We will ride into Barstow on the 16th -- I was assured that it is a secure location -- and catch the transport directly to the Hilton. There we will receive registration and accommodation passes, and then John can go down to the casino and lose all his money on the first night."

"Very funny," John said, not amused.

A waitress showed up with another round balanced on a vintage serving platter. Behind her came a confident-looking man in his forties, clean shaven and graying on top.

"Hi, folks. My name is Calvin Ale, the owner of this fine establishment. My staff has informed me that you are frequent customers and I would like to show my appreciation with a round on the house of our new Smoke Stack Stout. Hot off the presses."

He applied fresh coasters and moved the beers from the young lady's tray to our table with finesse.

"Well, thank you, Mr. Ale," Lucy said with a smile.

"Please call me Calvin, and be sure to let me know what you think of our Smoke Stack Stout," he said and bowed out.

John raised his glass. "A toast... to free beer." Glasses were raised and lowered.

"Anyone want some Macho Randy Savage nachos? I'm starving," John said.

We all ended up ordering food, picking off each other's plates and laughing the afternoon away. We tried to hold out for the band at 8:00, but 11% Smoke Stacks crept up on you. We went our separate ways in good cheer. Don and John never made the gun range, even though it was ladies' night. As a matter of fact, they never even mentioned it. We were still a month out from halibut season and I was feeling good about skipping out and actually spending that time with Lucy. This would be our first time together on her birthday and I had thought of the perfect gift. *****

Spring was upon us and the little rain the skies offered was welcomed. It helped to knock the dust down and make the oxygen more pleasant. The flowers around the beach house showed promise and the neighborhood took on an old-school feel. The asphalt on the roads had cracked and shifted slightly with the earth. Little wisps of grass worked as mortar holding it together. Roads were no longer needed, nor were they maintained. I liked it and enjoyed its character. Plus you could jog through the streets without being confined to the sidewalks and having to look over your shoulder at every sound.

Lucy and I were finishing up a long walk/run and were having some good afternoon conversation. We were both excited about the Expo and spending the summer together. We decided to Neuralink with some time to spare before our trip with Don and John. That way we could get used to it and maybe work some bugs out. We made the appointment for July 15$^{th}$. This would give us a good four weeks before we headed to Vegas.

"I don't want to tell anyone," Lucy said with a grin. "Let's see how long it is before someone notices."

"What about your mother?"

"Especially my mother. As soon as she knows, the world knows."

"What's so bad about that?"

"I don't know… it could be fun if we can control it like some twins can. I mean, think about it. A poker game, we could set each other up. Or raising kids, they couldn't play us against each other."

"Unless we have twins, then we are screwed. A family of mind games. Don and John are going to know something's up," I countered.

"We have to wait and see what happens, anyway. I just can't stop thinking about it."

"What do you want to do on your birthday this year?" I asked, trying to change the subject.

We weaved through the familiar neighborhood, almost home as she contemplated what she wanted. "I don't want a party, Ken. Let's just go to Traitor's for a nice steak and crab dinner and maybe stroll down the beach. Just the two of us."

"Your mom's not going to go for that."

"I'll tell her you are taking me out of town for the weekend."

"Traitor's it is, my sweet."

# Chapter Five

The rain was pounding on the steel roof above Dillon Maxwell. Drug withdrawal, alcohol dehydration and the down he felt after finishing his last victim and having the beautiful body removed from his possession, were all factors contributing to his skull being ripped apart with every exhale.

"Give me some H, goddamnit," he yelled through the industrial door to his office suite. He had taken two victims since the Houston girl was cut down early and filled with lead. Anger overwhelmed him and the void was not yet filled. Dillon opened one eye and was assaulted by the sun penetrating through the gap in the window shade. It moved back and forth with the air vent, continuing to jab its light into his eye like a reed of bamboo. His head was heavy and it was all he could do to roll over and put a stop to a fraction of the madness.

"H!" he screamed.
One of his men was already coming through the door.

"Chill, bro. Relax. Do you know what time it is? It's 8:30 in the morning. Everyone's still asleep."

Dillon did not respond with words. He would need this to function. He moved just enough to give his arm up for the needle. As the lava flowed through his veins he cinched his eyelids tighter and mumbled with a rasp, "Get out and wake everyone up."

Dillon liked his shop in Sedona and actually spent most of his time there. It had all a man could want, less women. He could not have women working for him. Temptation would be too great. His employees were forbidden to bring them to the shop or to hang pictures of them around. Dillon's other place of choice to reside was The Claiborne. A yacht currently docked off the coast of Fort Lauderdale. The plan was to wrap things up here, hit the Expo, and head for The Claiborne.

Dillon got to his feet and moved around a bit, ran the hot water of the shower over his neck for about 30 minutes and ventured down the stairs. He had a few things to check on and micromanage before the Expo. Time was ticking. The assembly of the launchers was a straight mass of parts in the east leg of the shop. His modified Ducati -- with a few parts off a Yamaha racer, composite plating and an arsenal of weapons -- occupied the adjacent pad. The living area at the center of the open floor plan was filled with ragged-looking men, tough as nails, and only awake at Dillon's request. The kitchen was at the bottom of the stairs where Jax greeted Dillon with a large cup of black coffee and a bottle of water. He downed the water like his life depended on it and glanced over at the crew. They immediately got up and moved to their respective stations of duty, breaking eye contact as soon as possible.

"You've got to cut 'em some slack, Dill," said Jax. He was the only one who could get away with cutting his name short. "They've been working late nights all month. Most of them never leaving and staying in the bunkers. Some of these guys have families, man. They know the deadline."

Dillon just stared at Jax for a moment without remorse. "Show me what we've got."

Jax gave Dillon the rundown. First an overview of the launcher production and then the tripods. Dillon was actually pleased with what he saw but held his emotions. It had been three days since the crew had seen Dillon and they were eager for his approval. That did not come easy. Dillon was a money maker. He ruled with an iron fist but rewarded his men well. He had killed for the launcher, taken the blueprints and had already produced a substantial number of units. He would triple his inventory before the Expo. This would put a larger target on his head, he knew, but money was power and power was his fuel. He would need to reinforce his security and use his head with every move. Things were about to happen for Dillon Maxwell.

"Let's check out the Ducati," he said with a little pep in his voice.

"You're going to love this," said Jax as they worked their way to the auto pad.

That area of the shop was spacious and organized. Walls full of parts, and fabrication stations for the ones they didn't have. Dillon was adamant about this being an in-house operation. It was in this area that he got his start. An apprentice at the ripe age of 12, Dillon was stripping vehicles to the bone and witnessing the transformations. Like a caterpillar to a butterfly, he used to say. The smell of the chop shop always resurrected his spotted memory of the good old days. Not much went on along those lines anymore as the profits were greater in other ways, but the shop would remain as an operational monument to his past.

"Ejection seats. What do you think of that, boss?" Jax said with confident hands on his hips, looking at the work in progress. "Depending on the altitude you can use these quick connects for oxygen," he said, pointing at the lines. "You've got to have your helmet on for ejection though. You hit this button with no helmet and you can kiss your ass goodbye."

"I'm listening and I'm liking," Dillon said, nodding his head.

Jax continued to point. "Flotation device, beacon, communication, accelerators, combat controls, kill switch. You follow me?"

"Go over the combat controls."

"I'm still working on the mount for the energy launcher, but the idea is thumb rotation here, screen number two. You have to switch over from grenades but you should have a 360-degree range with a heat lock."

"Nice. Did you do anything for protection at low altitude, when the field is weak?"

"When you come up on another field it would be hard to impact, but bullet deflection? No, the glass is bulletproof but the composite body can only deflect depending on speed." "What?" Dillon asked, puzzled.

"Listen. The shape is aggressive for combat. Most of the material is made up of composites that relax for turn and mobility, but contract to form a rigid body when accelerating. So, you want to be bulletproof at low altitude? Then I suggest you go full throttle."

"Is this going to be ready? If I can show the energy launcher operational on a glider, holy shit!"

"Ready to go. Locked and loaded."

"Jax, what the fuck are we going to call this thing? Energy Launcher sounds retarded."

"Let's call it the EL40. The capsules are 40 millimeters and the EL is for energy launcher. It's simple."

"Everything is simple to you. You make me sick, but good work."

\*\*\*\*\*

It was heating up outside, and combined with the never-ending dust, was becoming miserable. It made you just want to play out your days indoors. I was thankful that the humidity level was low. It made me think of my father. He refused to leave Pensacola, Florida. Once a Navy boy, always a Navy boy. He enjoyed watching the ships and staying close to the life. I had told him that San Diego would provide a similar lifestyle with better weather and closer to me, but 'if it ain't broke, don't fix it.'

I picked up my phone and scrolled to his image in my address book and thought, *I need to update his photo.* At 65 years of age, James Boyd Detrick did not look a day past 50, with close-cropped salt and pepper hair, always clean shaven, chiseled features, and impeccably dressed. He had not missed more than three straight days at the gym in the past 15 years, vacations included.

My mother was the one with the money. She went rogue from a royal family to wed a sailor and flee England. She was supposedly disowned from the estate for these actions but had kept in contact with her father, and for this, the money flowed. She was taken from us during a savage B&E, leaving a shell of a man with a bitter soul and wealth beyond means. Ten years had passed, and though my father had avenged her death by tracking the assailants and bringing them to justice by his hand, the hole in his heart would never be filled. But my father was a machine. He faced his fears every day, head-on. Got up each day like the rest of us, put on his shoes, and took part in the world of the living.

A ring and a half and he answered. "Kenny. What's up, tiger man?"

"I'm not five, Dad."

"I should hope not, knucklehead. What are you up to?" He was full of pet names. It drove me nuts, yet it was endearing.

"Just keeping in touch, old man. How's the weather there?"

"Swamp spit, but I've been through worse. When are you coming to see me? I need a cigar partner."

"Soon enough. Are you still seeing that little redhead number, Janet?"

"Yeah, she's still around, and then some." "Guess what?" I said with a quiet tone.

"Okay, what?"

"Lucy and I are going to Neuralink."

There was a pause on the line. "You're fucking stupid."

I paused back. "Yeah, I kind of feel the same way, but I'm kind of excited and I had to tell someone. Are you telling me if Mom was here today that you guys wouldn't do it?"

"Ken, I've seen a lot of solid relationships ruined over this. You think you're strong enough, let a woman in your head. So to answer your question, hell no. But I'm sure you've done your research and I wish the best for you."

"Well… thanks for nothing, Scrooge," I said. "Guess what else?"

"You have a newfound love of daffodils?"

"We are going to the Expo," I said, ignoring his comment.

"Nice. I wouldn't be caught dead over there. Way too many people. None of that shit interests me anyway. Maybe the fights, but I can watch those from the comforts of my leather."

"They have really stepped up the security around the square and we don't plan to venture out. Don and John got the tickets comp'd from one of their clients."

"Well, sounds like things are going good for you, bud. I've got to cut you off now, racquetball in fifteen." "All right Dad, don't be a stranger. Love you."

"Love you too, moose." Click.

*****

Forty minutes later I set my Batmobile down outside the Santa Monica plaza. Mike's camera shop was a blast from the past. Set right in the middle of modern mania. I made my way through the youth, giving off a few *don't fuck with it* looks referring to my Ducati glider that I parked nearby. I think one noticed the shotgun when my duster opened slightly. Oops. I found the elevators and rose to the seventh floor. The plaza was an open design spiraling up like a smokestack. The thought made me thirsty, mmm. Flags protruded from each level -- I think to prevent vertigo -- but maybe they were for the jumpers to grab hold of should they change their mind mid-flight. The doors slid open to Mike's and I went back in time.

"You must be Mike," I said to the old man with the white handlebar mustache.

"That's what the sign says."

"I'm Ken. I called about the Nikon."

His posture changed and he came out of his shell. His voice went up an octave as he spoke. "Ultra-wide angle with zoom, high precision, spherical lens for sharpness?"

I could hear the life being restored in his voice. "That's the one," I said as I approached the counter.

"Got it right here, came in last night. I was worried a bit. Thought you might not show. I should have taken a deposit for peace of mind."

"Well, don't fret. By golly, I'm here," I said in my best Gomer Pyle voice.

He started punching on a register that I wouldn't doubt was forty years older than I am. I was floored.

"Hood, tick; case, tick; cap, tick; extra memory card, tick; body, tick; lens, tick." He rattled off all the things that come with a camera of this magnitude.

"Holy shit, captain, don't you have a package price or something?"

"Name's Mike, and this is a cash price, mate."
I could tell this man was all business when it came down to brass tacks. "What's the damage, Mike?"

"Six thousand four hundred ninety-five dollars and ninetynine cents," he said with a 'you got the deal of a century' tone.

I paid the man and felt good about doing it. Not only was Lucy going to be ecstatic about it, but Old Man River's heart was beating again.

*****

"Here you go, boss. Just came in," Grant said. He spread out the disks on the coffee table so Dillon could examine them.

Dillon had given Grant the task, knowing he would come through. Grant had always been his go-to man for betting and finances. He had acted as his bookie and made Dillon a lot of money over the years. His advice was sound and his experience had been invaluable. This year's main mixed martial arts event was to take place at the Expo in Las Vegas. Grant had suggested Dillon do his homework.

"This is the largest purse ever for a single fight," said Grant. "And is planned to bring booking numbers that will rival that of the Super Bowl."

"Is there some kind of chronological order here?" asked Dillon, looking at the disks.

"I left some of the dates off on purpose. Why don't you start with this current training footage? I've found it works best this way. If you start in the beginning, with the early stuff, you could develop a favorite based on likability. This is not a reality show where popularity is the key. Nothing good can come from this, Dillon." He paused and looked him in the eyes. "Leave emotions out of it."

"Do I look like I'll have a problem with that?"

"Just concentrate on technique. Get a feel for aggression, yet control. Who wants it more, Dillon? Then that's your man."

Grant got up and put a training disk in and excused himself. Dillon watched the footage several times. Pausing to look in battered eyes, rewinding moves, over and over again, leaving no stone unturned. He studied their facilities, who they trained with, friends, family. These guys were animals, and on a certain level, Dillon could relate.

## Tale of the Tape

| Cole "The Real Deal" Severn | | James "The Kraken" Montel |
|---|---|---|
| 31 | Age | 25 |
| 6'3" | Height | 6'5" |
| 225 lbs | Weight | 225 lbs |
| 77" | Reach | 84" |
| Striker/Jujitsu | Style | Striker/ Muay-Thai |
| 39-0 | Record | 40-1-1 |
| 30 in the 1st round | | 32 in the 1st round |

Dillon was leaning toward The Kraken. The height and reach advantage were obvious. His vicious elbows and Muay-Thai clinch seemed to be unstoppable, but anything could happen. The Real Deal was lightning quick, and if the fight went to the ground his strength could be the factor. This was a very difficult decision. For three days Dillon got to know the fighters. He found himself liking The Real Deal, but his money would be with The Kraken.

"Grant, let's talk," Dillon shouted over his shoulder. Grant took a seat and waited for Dillon to continue. "You putting money on this fight?"

"Of course," Grant said without elaborating.

"Well, who do you got?"

"Don't let me sway you. I wouldn't want to face the music."

They were silent for Dillon's last seconds of contemplation. "$1.5 million… on The Kraken."

Dillon's look was dead serious and Grant did not question. He nodded as if to say, *done,* and rose to his feet.

"Grant," Dillon said to stop him. "Who do you got?"

"The Kraken. I could have told you that three days ago."

# Chapter Six

The morning was gloomy and gray. I remembered the days of summer, sun, bikinis, and volleyball. I could sit on my porch and people-watch all day. Now, just a few die-hard surfers were in the distance. The pier still attracted people because the sand and dust was not as bad out over the water, but excitement was in the air at my homestead. Lucy was running around snapping photos with her new toy. She was ecstatic and could not put it down.

"I just can't get over the shutter speed and the low aperture," she said and played with the lens adjustments.

"You're talking Greek to me baby, but I'm glad you like it," I said.

"I was talking with Chrissy the other day, you remember, my roommate from college?" she said.

"Yes, my love. I know who she is. You don't have to remind me that she was your college roommate every time you mention her."

"Well, guess what? She's going to be at the Expo. Her company is sending her as one of their representatives and she wants to hang out. She can't wait to meet you."

"I'm so excited..." I said in a girlish tone and a smirk on my face.

"You're going to love her. She knows all about you."

I squinted my eyes and studied her face. "You told her, didn't you?"

"Told her what?"

"Don't play coy with me. You told her about the Neuralink?"

"Maybe," she said slowly.

"I knew you would tell someone, but I just figured it would be your mother."

She squinted her eyes back at me and replied, "You told your dad, didn't you?"

"Maybe."

She came over and sat on my lap and put her arms around my shoulders. "You are such a hypocrite."

"You're the one who wanted to keep it a secret." "I love you," she said and kissed me deeply.

Lucy got up and I slapped her on the ass. "Pack an overnight bag," I said. "I booked a room for us tomorrow night. I figured after the procedure we could chill out for a bit and see what transpires."

"Sounds great. What time are we leaving again?

"Six sharp, takes a few hours to get there and our appointment is at 9:30, unless you want to back out?"

"Fat chance, Charlie Brown," she replied and giggled.

We left right on time the next morning and headed for the closest Neuralink facility for our birthday into a new world. The old Siltec Silicon plant in Huntsville, Texas had been converted into a modern marvel that was now housing the headquarters of Neuralink Technologies.

We walked through the doors with nerves twitching and were professionally greeted and shown to a waiting room with a very clinical feel. Lucy had a permanent grin on her face and she was as beautiful as ever.

"Okay. I think we have a brief consultation, some liability forms to fill out and then we sign our lives away. I hear it's worse than buying a house," I said to Lucy.

"I can't believe we are doing this."

"We can't let this backfire, Lucy. We need to promise to keep an open mind and attitude toward one another."

"I promise, Ken. I love you more than life."

She leaned in and kissed me for more reassurance, and I knew I was ready.

We sat down and listened to the clinician explain the procedure and what we could expect. She explained that there would be two follow up appointments within the first year to get feedback and record brain activity.

"These are very basic tests," she stated factually. "How you two link exactly is unpredictable. There are a variety of ways our clients have connected. The most common link experienced is within your dreams. Even this area can be a little hazy though. In most cases we have found that partners are just experiencing the exact same dream."

A man walked into the room. He had aging features and signs of stress had scarred his face, yet his hands were steady as steel.

"Meet Dr. Snyder, one of the co-founders of the Neuralink Corporation. He will be overseeing your procedure today," she said.

"Carry on," Dr. Snyder said as he took a seat to observe.

"There have been reports of shared pains," she continued. "It is rare to feel each other's physical pain, but it isn't unheard of. For example, a hockey player took a stick shot to his leg and his partner didn't feel this pain at the time, but the next morning her leg was severely bruised and so sore she could not walk for several days. But like I said, this was an extreme case. As well as in dreams, sharing traumas, anxieties, fears and stimulations are areas that are also fairly common. For example, a train strikes Lucy while you're sitting at home having a beverage. You might experience the spike in adrenaline that ran through her body just before impact, but you won't know exactly what happened. You'll know something happened, and you'll feel it."

"I know you can't predict our case but is it possible we will be able to read each other's thoughts?" Lucy asked.

"Possibly, it's more like sharing the same thoughts. In some cases a telepathic-like communication has been reported, but the studies are showing that it's just two minds thinking alike. You might look at each other and nod your head because you're thinking the same thing, so you know what he's thinking. Does that make sense?"

"I guess so," Lucy said, not quite sure of herself.

"In any case, you will have to wait and see. Grow with each other and enjoy it. You won't regret it."

Lucy looked at me and winked. What we were told came as no surprise. We were ready and knew that sometimes you just had to throw caution to the wind and ignore your fears. Good things were to come… Or so we thought.

She showed us to the procedure room and introduced us to the staff. Dr. Snyder was studying the monitors while we took our seats in the middle of the room. I felt like a test dummy strapped to an electric chair. They strategically placed electrode pads on our heads and used a thin bandage wrap to keep them tight against our scalp. Shaving was not a requirement. They probably figured that people wouldn't do it if they had to shave their heads for the procedure. Then they placed a simple warming sock over our heads. We looked like thugs with wire dreadlocks under our skull caps.

"Hey, Lucy. Photo op," I said and was warmed with a smile.

"Here goes nothing," she said.

Small pulses abruptly changed our focal points. I could feel my face twitching as they intensified, my eyes rolling back in their sockets. My eyes watered instantly and I could feel my head sweating under the cap. Sensations of movement came on like my body was in motion through a vigorous maze of geometrical patterns. Atoms raced like pulsating static. Cold enveloped. Spikes of light rapidly penetrated my retinas as the smell of copper filled my nostrils just before the lights went out.

When I awoke it was all over. Thirty minutes had gone by like a flash of light and a roar of thunder. I felt slightly better than I expected. Like I had a restless night of sleep with a nightmare or two. I thought, *just another hangover to kick*. I blinked my eyes a few times. My lids felt heavy as I looked over at Lucy. Her beautiful blue eyes stared back at me. Glossy and a little tired, but exotic. She mouthed the words *I love you.*

We laid there together in the recovery room, in and out of sleep, for the next couple of hours. A nurse entered the room. She spoke clear and fast, like a wham-bam-thank-you-ma'am type of speech.

"Okay guys, you're good. Vitals are stable and you are free to go. Please schedule your follow up with Katie at the front desk and have a great day."

"Excuse me," I said, stopping her for a moment, "How do you know our vitals are stable?"

"Oh, yes. The transmitters feed us the information we need."

I gave her a skeptical look.

"This room is designed to record algorithms through radio waves. It shows us breathing rates, heartbeats, murmurs, brain activity, muscle spasms, even goose bumps; and if you blink your eyes we know it."

"How the hell does it do that?" Lucy asked.

"I don't know exactly, but I've been told there are about thirty little radio transmitters sending waves to each station. I guess they bounce back off you, feeding the detectors your information." She shrugged her shoulders and bolted out the door.

Lucy and I just looked at each other and shook our heads.

"Wow, let's get going, love bug," she said. I held the door for her and placed my hand in the small of her back to guide her out.

Twenty minutes later we checked into the Courtyard Hotel, but we didn't see any courtyards. I inserted my little plastic card key and the light blinked red. Lucy and I both chuckled. We looked at each other and spoke simultaneously, "every fucking time." We both busted up laughing like schoolgirls. I flipped the key, got a green light and Lucy pushed me through the door to the bed.

"Don't talk, just think," she said. She placed her forehead against mine and stared into my eyes. I'm sure I looked as much like a Cyclops as she did to me.

"What are you thinking, Cyclops?" she said, breaking the silence.

"I thought you didn't want me to talk. But I'm thinking your eye is beautiful."

We laughed again and her lips touched mine. We felt like two young kids in the back seat at a drive-in. At almost forty it was amazing.

We headed out to get a bite after having the most vigorous and intense sexual experience of our lives. It was as if she knew exactly what I wanted and when, and I knew what she wanted. We truly felt bonded, and cloud nine was our playground. We were famished from traveling, the Neuralink procedure and the amazing sex, and we needed to refuel. *Greasy cheeseburger it is*, we agreed without audio.

Over the next couple of weeks we put ourselves through a series of tests. Just to try and get a grip on our situation. Our largest obstacle was to keep from laughing or making it look like we were sharing an inside joke every two minutes. This we found to be difficult, but not impossible.

It was a couple of nights before Don and John returned from Alaska, and Lucy and I experienced the same dream. It was a little abstract -- as dreams should be -- but there was no doubt that we linked. The ocean swells were huge. Massive 40- to 50-foot drops and our small fishing boat was up and down on them like a roller coaster. The perfect storm. I was riding it out curled up in the fetal position on the floor of the cabin. I had never had motion sickness in my life, but dreams will be dreams. I looked up and saw Lucy holding on to the wooden bench seat in the nook. She thought this whole thing was funny.

"Oh sweetheart, you are such a Nancy, my big strong man," she said, having a ball at my expense.

John poked his head into the cabin as ice-cold water broke over his shoulders and crashed to the planked floor. He didn't even flinch. "You don't want to be down here, guys. We're taking on a lot of water. If she fragments with you in the belly you won't have a prayer."

Don was in the captain's chair and calm as can be. They all shared in a laugh when I crawled out from below and flopped on the deck like a dead fish. John handed me a beer and said, "Here's to getting your cherry popped."

The boat was still and the waters were calm. The sun was shining like it could only do in a dream. The clouds were puffy white cotton balls with a silver lining, brushed on a baby blue backdrop. *Only in a photo*, I thought. Lucy was thinking the same thing and was bummed she didn't have her camera. She was laid out on the stern in a yellow polka dot bikini, soaking in the rays. She looked at me and smiled.

John caught the look we shared and said, "What the fuck is going on? You two are acting very funny."

We looked at John, then back to each other. *Don't break, Lucy. Don't laugh. Hold it, hold it.* Bam. We both cracked up with snorting laughter.

"Don. What do you think, bro? These two got some explaining to do or what?" John said.

"I would say so there, Johnnie, there's something fishy going on here."

"I don't know what you're talking about," I said.

With perfect timing a large humpback whale broke the surface of the water along with the tension in the air. She sideswiped the boat and Lucy, Don and John joined me on the deck against their will. Don was quickly to his feet in pure excitement.

"Look at that beauty. You know what this means?" he said.

I looked at Lucy and whispered, "That the light is off of us."

Don continued, "It's good luck for the season. It means that she gives her consent to fish her waters. When a female kisses a boat without capsizing it, it brings good fortune. We'll have no problem cutting two weeks off this year."

Lucy and I shared a smile and the dream faded with Don and John high fiving in the distance.

We talked about our dreams every morning since we were linked. We had been disappointed that we didn't have any similarities. Then she mentioned the dream about the boat and we knew we had had the exact same dream. Feelings, thoughts, and the high five were all the same. It was surreal and freaky at the same time. We felt our link evolving.

Two days later, the night before Vegas, we met up with Don and John to hear about their excursion and to go over our travel plans. There was no sighting of a kissing whale, but the trip was successful and their cousin Rocky worked out well and wanted to return for the next season. All of their quotas were going to be met.

Lucy and I were doing good at keeping our little secret until she started asking questions.

"Have you guys shared dreams? Do you still?" she asked.

"That's kind of personal, Lucy," John said. "Don has a lot of wet dreams. He just won't admit it."

"Very funny," Don said "At least mine are with the opposite sex, you gay blade."

"Okay. Forget I asked that one," she said, holding her hands up.

I gave Lucy a look and tried to will her to stop this line of questioning.

"We have had the same dreams before. Mostly when we were young, but we kind of grew out of it," Don said. "Or it might be that we just quit talking about them."

"Well, you guys never really spoke about this before, but, I don't know… Do you guys connect, and in what ways?" Lucy asked.

"We don't talk much about it because growing up, that's all we did," John said. "Talk, talk, talk, talk, talk. I'm stupid now because my brain has been shrunk by idiot shrinks, over and over, for the first two decades of my life."

"Let's just change the subject," I said. I needed a Long Island.

"It's all right, Ken," Don said with a voice of reason. "When we were young -- around 5th or 6th grade -- they started with the chess games. Over and over we played. Neither one of us really dominated the other. Now, John being stupid and all, it might be a different story."

John puffed his chest up a bit.

"It was a test as well as a training tool. Mind control or manipulation of one another's thought patterns. We share the same neural pathways, but can we will each other's pattern to change?" Don said. "The answer is yes, and it's in this area that John and I excel. Basically I can make him take the garbage out."

"And I can make Don fuck his cat," John said, without missing a beat.

"You can see how this ability will take us nowhere," Don said. "So we called it a truce and vowed to never play chess again. Meaning, he stays out of my head and I stay out of his."

The waitress must have overheard our conversation as she brought over a Long Island and with a giggle, placed it in front of me. "Would you like a sissy stick, hon?" Noticing the roll of my eyes she turned her attention. "What will the rest of you have?"

Orders were placed, food and drinks were consumed and Lucy's line of questioning changed. She was hoping for some positive feedback, but the well was dry thanks to the much needed interruption. We mostly talked about the Expo and listened to the twins pick at each other. Two and a half months on a 38-foot boat made them short-tempered, but then again, are they ever really apart?

We parted when the skies darkened, and agreed to just meet in Barstow at the 5-Alarm secured parking facility. We would catch the 12:00 transportation shuttle and arrive at the Hilton Towers in Las Vegas early that afternoon.

# Chapter Seven

The Expo was massive. No other way to describe it. The skies of Las Vegas were flooded with traffic, blocking what little light the sun offered. The city was lit by the illuminating structures and signs as well as the hovercrafts. The dust was constant and could be tasted with every breath. People from all over the world would settle down into the casinos by the thousands. The event was of international scale, bringing together a variety of expositions for two straight weeks, 24 hours a day.

The festivities began with SEMA (Specialty Equipment Market Association) bringing the brightest minds in the world together with extraordinary product lines shown in action. There were exhibits from Universal Studios showing the industry's evolution. Space Exposition displayed the latest technological advancements in NASA. As well as gun shows with everything from antiques to modern military arms and strategies. It was a Sturgis-like rally for enthusiasts and casual passersby alike. Something for everyone, whether it was Honda, Suzuki, BMW, Ducati, or Piaggiano. They all showcased their old and new products: Choppers, Cruisers, Falcons, and Gladiators. If you had a product, this was the place. Everything from MMA to Neuralink was going to be at the Expo. Pure chaos, but something everyone must experience at least once in their life.

Dillon rolled in deep to set up camp at Planet Hollywood adjacent to the Hilton Towers. The roof retracted and swallowed up his entire entourage. Dillon was there for business. Usually he liked to partake in races, concerts and casinos, but this time he would catch the MMA super fight since he had money riding on it, conduct his business with Mr. Portman and get the hell out of dodge.

Dillon looked over at Jax as they secured their crafts and cargo. "Go check on the doctor. Make sure there are no complications," he ordered.

*****

We found seats in the transportation shuttle across from the twins. Lucy and I laughed at the same time.

"What are you two smirking about?" John said.

"Let's just switch places," Lucy said to John. We couldn't make them ride that way. They needed two seats apiece. If Lucy and I both took one of them as a partner they might just make it to Vegas without killing each other.

John nodded and rolled his eyes to the door as he sat down, prodding me with his elbow. I looked to my left at a couple of skirts, as John would say, entering the shuttle. Some unaccompanied men quickly made room in their section for the newcomers, forcing a sigh from John's lungs. Lucy just shook her head in a typical 'you're a juvenile' fashion.

"How long is this ride again?" John asked.

"I think you can show some restraint, Pepe," Don said. "There will be more than enough tail to chase in Vegas."

I looked around, scanning from seat to seat, getting a feel for our riding companions. There were some unsavory looking characters aboard but nothing to be concerned about. Overall, I felt pretty secure with the 5-Alarm facility and transportation.

The shuttle came to life with a confident hum as a female voice -- with sex appeal, as John pointed out -- gave flight instructions. "Good morning. Welcome aboard 5-Alarm shuttle service to and from Las Vegas, Nevada. Please refrain from smoking, keep your seatbelts firmly fastened and all weapons properly secured on safety mode. And thank you again for securing your vehicles with 5-Alarm."

"What. We just can't smoke? This is going to be a party," John blurted out.

No one thought it was funny. People shifted around, securing weapons and carry-ons. Even the skirts appeared to be packing. This clearly wasn't the party bus John was hoping for. When you confine strangers in a box, people get on edge. Vegas would be different, with room to breathe and alcohol to consume.

Most of the ride would lack friendly conversation, but we all had one thing in common, the Expo. And it was on all of our minds as the shuttle lifted off and got to full speed within minutes. Buildings blurred by the windows and quickly turned to sand streaked with cacti resembling pond algae across moving water. *What lies ahead? Hopefully, the experience of a lifetime.*

The shuttle muscled its way into the city using size and weight to push smaller hovercraft aside, and lowered to the landing pad at the top of the towers.

"Wow... Now that's service," Don said as we tipped for our baggage.

We shuffled into the golden express elevators and were shot down through the structure in a matter of seconds, bypassing ten floors with every blink.

Lucy was excited, I could tell. She was anxious and full of energy, snapping photos of the lobby ceiling, marble floors and the ornate fountains. She had never stayed in luxury. Her emotions transferred to me and fueled the day.

John was already eyeing the casino. "Down, boy," Don said.

It took three hours to check into our rooms, but time did not matter as we were in good company and a cocktail waitress had found a gold mine in us.

Lucy was combing through an Expo magazine and spotted the Severn/Montel fight. "Look at these guys. They're huge," she said.

"The photos make 'em look big," John said. "You should know that, Miss Photographer."

"Look, they're only 225 pounds, they're itty bitty guys," Don said. "They wouldn't have a prayer against my 357."

"I'm sorry. I didn't mean to step on your ego. You are the almighty," she said with sarcasm. "I'm sure they would cower at your mere presence."

"Thank you, apology accepted."

We made our way to our rooms to settle in and ready ourselves for the evening. Lucy took a call as I was exploring the mini bar like a child in a candy shop.

"Well, hang on a second. Let me see what Ken thinks," she said and put her cell phone to her chest.

She looked at me and grinned. I squinted my right eye and studied her for a second.

"She has tickets?" I said. "Maybe… the Severn/Montel fight?"

Lucy nodded her head. "Really good ones, too. Her company has a block of floor seats and some people backed out, I guess."

"So, all four of us?" I asked.

She nodded her head and went to back to talking.

Don and John half knocked on the door and barged into our room.

"What the fuck, truck?" I said.

"Have you ever heard of a lock? There are some crazy MF'ers out there," Don said. He tossed a shotgun on the bed and heaved his bulk next to it. John straddled the desk chair and started thumbing through our mini bar.

I shook my head. "You guys want to see the fights tomorrow night?" I asked.

"I figured we would catch them on the jumbo-tron in the casino," Don replied.

"No, I mean floor seats. Lucy has a connection."

"Does a bear shit in the woods?" John said.

"Hell, yeah. That's been sold out for months, bro." "How much we talkin'?" Don asked.

"If she wants any compensation, I got it. Don't worry about it. Besides, it sounds like it's company funded."

"She? Well, then count us in, my friend. Do you have any idea what floor seats run?" Don said. "Who is this wonder woman and what company does she work for?"

"My guess is about fifteen hundred a butt pad. I think she is a producer and model. One of the bikini clads with high powered rifles and Uzis."

"You mean Portman Industries?" Don asked.

I raised my eyebrows to confirm.

"Holy shit," said John. "I'm going to have to shave my chest again."

*****

Ray rapped on the door to Dillon's suite, put his ear to the steel and heard footsteps. "It's Ray, let me in," he said.

The door opened and Enriquez holstered his weapon. Ray stepped aside, parting the way for a beautiful woman. His eyes drifted and lingered on her hips as she crossed the marble foyer.

"Stop," Dillon said with a commanding tone. He drew on an anniversary edition Patron cigar, puffed out his cheeks for the tobacco, turned his chair from the window and glared with penetrating eyes as he exhaled.

"I think she's a winner, boss," Ray said, taking a seat at the bar.

Dillon's eyes moved to Ray just long enough for Ray to break the contact. He moved his stare back to the female and relished in feeling her skin crawl.

"Move a little closer, slowly," Dillon said.

She moved, trying to keep her grace, though her adrenaline spiked.

"Good. Now turn around, hon. Let me see what you've got."

She rotated slowly, hiking out her hip and blowing a seductive kiss. She was stunning, with long dark hair, coral green eyes, olive skin, naturally swollen lips. Her gunmetal grey onepiece hugged her body, accentuating every curve.

"Say something. Let me hear you speak," Dillon said. She had the look, but did she have the intellect for the job, was the question.

"My name is Shelby, I'm 22-years-old, bleed red, white and blue and am an activist for the NRA," she said. "I mean, I'm Carla, baby," switching her accent at will. "One hundred twenty pounds of pure adrenaline junky. Let's go jump out of a plane over the canyon."

She held Dillon's watching stare and felt a shiver through her bones. She couldn't hold on, diverted her gaze and pretended to admire the room as Dillon rose from his chair. She wanted to leave… and leave now. This man made her very uneasy, but money talks.

Dillon put the cigar down and approached the girl.

"What is your name, sweetheart?" he asked with a 'don't even think of lying' tone.

"Cory," she said under her breath.

Dillon took her hand and brought it up to his face. Pressing his nose to her knuckles he drew in her scent. "Ralph Lauren," he said. "Very sharp, sassy for a girl like you. Is it Safari?"

"Very good," she said.

"Don't wear it that night. Put on something more exotic. Like Euphoria or Obsession from Calvin Klein. Understand?"
"No problem."

He continued to breathe her in as he ran his face up her arm and over her bare shoulder to the small of her neck. She leaned her face away and felt her knees start to give.

Dillon let her arm go and walked back to his cigar.

"Cory, my dear, we will have the mark back within an hour. You are to stay in that room the whole time, is that clear?"

"Yes sir, no problem."

"He will be out for a bit when he is returned. No one can come in. Three hours tops from beginning to end. He must awaken on his own accord and leave satisfied. This is very important." Dillon paused for effect. "Ray will fill you in if you have further questions."

Dillon looked at Enriquez and used his eyes to point to the door. Enriquez secured the hallway and Ray escorted her out, once again admiring her swaying hips.

Dillon blew smoke rings as he stood staring out over the strip. "Let's go over the contract one more time," he said to Patrick, who was sitting silent, enjoying a cigar of his own.

"We've been over this, Dillon. It's perfect."

"Just bring it up. I want to recheck the account numbers too."

Patrick worked his magic and a virtual screen manifested over the coffee table, displaying the contract in question.

"Don't you want to go roll some dice or something? It's really the only night we have, Dillon. See some of the exhibits? Check out some ladies?"

"This is a business trip, Patty. We'll see plenty of girls at the fights tomorrow night, I'm sure. Right now we have to stay focused. Go check on Tom and make sure all the rotations are covered. I don't want any surprises tonight."

*****

The night was young and John was itching to gamble in one way or another. Don and I wanted to check out the Modern Marvels exhibit and Lucy was stuck on The Evolution of Universal Studios, her love of cameras and all. Our minds were differing, maybe through all the commotion and excitement.

But one thing we all agreed upon was to stay together, at least within the same building. This event brought out all walks of life and you could be sure that some had bad intentions. Every man, woman and child was sure to be packing some sort of heat. Security was run by the individual businesses and was confined to their properties. If it didn't affect their bottom line, it wasn't an issue. Violence was met by violence and the trash would be removed to the next neutral zone or disposed of altogether. Where security was heavy, incidents were typically low. These people didn't mess around. So we stayed within the main structures and John promised to keep his gambling to the bottom of The Towers.

The center of the Expo was referred to as the square. It sectioned off a large portion of the strip, incorporating the front of the Bellagio casino. Security was abundant there and no one got in without a pass. A yellow neon badge stood out on the black combat gear held together by bold stitched neon seams, identifying the abundant security staff. And even with the sea of people, the reflective yellow was always in sight.

We just took it all in, enjoying the music, live shows and excellent food. They offered shuttle rides to and from the main attractions, running 24 hours a day. Every direction you looked you could catch a digital marquee advertising events, locations and times. There would be no way for us to cover the entire show. We confirmed our bearings and worked out a plan of action to minimize our traveling time.

We decided to have a few drinks at one of the clubs in The Towers while John went out to lose some money. Lucy's friend Chrissy and a few of her colleagues stopped by to drop off the tickets for the fight. Don was floored by Chrissy and so was I. She was aging, like us. But at nearly 40, beauty and brains held their own. Lucy took some pictures of her and her girls to show John. You could tell they were no strangers to the lens. He was going to be pissed he had missed them. And we would hear his drunken whine.

*****

Chrissy had attended CSU at the same time as Lucy. They shared the living expenses during their junior and senior years in a small two bedroom, over the garage apartment less than a mile from campus. Chrissy had the figure and the brains. She had done some modeling through college for local calendars, some low-end clothing lines and the occasional bridal show. That is how Lucy met her. Cover shot for the CSU calendar, beach theme. Lucy had happily drawn the shoot. Of course the cover girl got all of the notoriety.

Upon graduation Chrissy disappeared into a world far different than Lucy. Chrissy went to work for Portman Industries, the largest arms dealer in the world, leaving Lucy in the dust with her camera in hand. She was employed for her looks but moved up through the ranks with her street savvy, yet educated business mind. What she does for Portman Industries in entirety is unknown, but on the outside she successfully runs the advertising portion worldwide. Everything from catalogs, to brochures, to calendars, to live demos. Running a crew of hundreds, every one as beautiful as the next. She poses her ladies in some of the most extreme corners of the world with the most extreme arsenal of weapons in hand; clothing is often not part of the equation.

# Chapter Eight

The mixed martial arts event of the century was about to commence. The facility was owned by the UFC (Ultimate Fighting Championship) enterprise. But in actuality was just an extension of the MGM Grand hotel and casino. We entered the massive arena through the east doors. Lights were blazing about the crowd, illuminating faces and pulsating to the base that assaulted our ears and vibrated our solo cups containing $15 worth of watered barley apiece.

"Hopefully we can get some better drinks down there on the floor," John shouted.

"I don't even know how to get down there," I responded.

The crowd was half standing, gyrating to the music and consuming alcohol by the tons. John pointed down towards event staff and we snaked our way through the masses.

The lights went out and an earsplitting siren stopped us in our tracks as lasers lit up the octagon battle platform in the center of the arena. The pattern of the rapid-changing laser beams formed a ten-foot-tall hologram-like figure of the announcer. The siren stopped and his voice thundered. "Ladies and gentlemen. Take… your… seats," he said, raising both hands in the air.

The floor lights came on low and Lucy squeezed my hand to continue moving. Two laser figures of fighters appeared over the crowd on opposite sides of the octagon. They were large but lifelike, with digital sweat pouring off their bodies and dissipating just before hitting the spectators below. They were moving to the music with punching motions and footwork, while the tale of the tape was read and projected behind each one like a vapor trail following them to battle. They lowered to the octagon and slowly shrank to life size along with the announcer. The laser images were replaced with the real fighters by a flash of light and some old fashioned pyrotechnics.

"That was fucking cool," shouted John, "and these are just the prelims."

"No kidding," said Lucy. "There. Grab him."

She was pointing to a large brick of a man with *Staff* written across his chest. He escorted us to our seats and we put Don and John on the outside for leg room. When Chrissy showed up with her girls, we all stood to let them in. John went slackjawed and mumbled his hellos. He tried to follow them to the center of the row and Lucy stopped him with a scolding finger.

"Sit down, Pee-wee Herman," she said.

He looked at her and scuffed like a child. "Yes, ma'am," he said, returning to his seat.

Crack. Right cross and a fighter hit the coated chain link face first. I swear I felt a speck of blood hit me. I wiped my cheek and downed my drink.

"Grab that waitress when she comes by," I said to John.

"One step ahead of you, bro," he replied.

People were still pouring in and a lot of the floor seats remained empty. This area was often reserved for bigwigs who only wanted to see the main cards, or family and fight camp personnel who came and went with the fighters.

Next up were a couple of grapplers. This often made for a good stand up situation as both men would respect their opponent's ground game. This was not the case. The bout turned into a drawn out wrestling match that was approaching decision time.

Alexander Portman entered the floor area with his entourage of beautiful people and filled the rest of the section. He paid no mind to us and was engulfed in conversation with his hired hands.

"He would make a great James Bond," I said to Lucy.

"From what Chris tells me, he is James Bond," she replied.

A couple more fights went by. Each one announced in the same laser light show fashion. I could feel some tension among the Portman staff to my left and noticed a few men step into our section and stand over Alexander. He started to rise and one of the men placed a hand on his shoulder, restricting him. Security did not intervene, nor did his muscle. But I could tell they were at the ready. A tall barrel of a man with a five o'clock shadow squatted down next to Alexander and looked straight ahead as he spoke, "Mr. Portman, my name is Dillon Maxwell. I believe you know who I am and what I have. It will be in your best interest to meet with me for a friendly proposition. I have reserved the Encore Room immediately following the main event. Please join me." He got up, cast a glance in our direction, lingered his retinas uncomfortably on Lucy and walked away.

The third and final bell rang -- decision time -- for the judges as well as Mr. Alexander Portman.

"Who the hell was that?" Lucy said. "He looked right at me."

"I don't have a clue," I said, shaking my head.

The audience roared for their favorite fighter as they prepared to announce the decision. Dillon and his men took their seats a few rows up and a couple of sections over. Still an excellent view. Dillon leaned into Jax, "Did you spot the blond with the blue dress?"

Jax nodded once to confirm.

"Good," Dillon said. He took one last look at the back of Lucy's head then turned his attention to the octagon.

The fights continued, some inside the ring and some outside. Both were thoroughly entertaining. The ones within the fence ended with sportsman-like hugs while the others were quickly smothered by staff and removed with professional precision.

We were all intoxicated by the time they announced the main event, but not to the point of memory loss. We were going to enjoy this. The lights dropped once more but remained out a bit longer this time. Music trampled through the air as the lasers struck the audience and rotated clockwise around the arena. It felt like we were being pulled through a vortex to another world. A world where savage beasts eat their young and are bred to battle to the death in cages.

The lasers moved together, creating the figures of James, "The Kraken," Montel and his opponent Cole, "The Real Deal," Severn. The virtual fighters continued moving clockwise above our heads with a grapevine foot pattern, staring into each other's souls from across the void. The decibel level of the drunken fans rose to just below ear shattering. It was a spectacular view as the fighters came together in the octagon head to head.

The announcer rattled off the tale of the tape as we witnessed a bloodthirsty pre-fight stare down. The fighters appeared in the flesh out of nowhere and were silhouetted by their respective holograms. The lasers moved with their motion as if it was choreographed and did not dissipate until the first punch was thrown.

The battle was bloody, as promised. The Kraken's elbows were too fast for the not-so-Real Deal, splattering crimson with each connection. Severn was able to get hold of him from time to time but always ended up on the bottom. Montel's reach allowed him to post up and rain down punches. He was unstoppable. TKO - two minutes, forty seconds into the second round. Severn had had enough and stopped defending himself, succumbing to defeat.

The Kraken rose to his feet and raised both fists high in the air for a victory roar. The lasers cast over him, making him seem immortal and vicious beyond belief. With Cole's blood dripping from his elbows to the mat, he circled and bored his death stare into each and every one of us. He was captivating until the last moment.

Light penetrated through the exits as the crowd ungracefully dissipated. Alexander Portman and his posse were gone like ghosts, never having the courtesy of introduction. I was thankful for the seats, nonetheless.

*****

"Mr. Portman, have a seat, please," Dillon said with as much politeness as he could muster.

"I prefer to stand," Portman said, looking Dillon in the eyes.

The tension was pungent in the room. Dillon was seated on one side of a large, clear, cherry wood slab table with several of his men perched behind him, facing the doorway.

"Suit yourself," he said.

"I am aware of who you are, Mr. Maxwell, and I have some questions for you as well."

"Shoot."

"Poor choice of words. Where did you get it?"

"That is of no consequence to you."

"Where is Mr. Jax? Will he be joining us?"

"He and Grant are retrieving my money at this time. How is it that you know so much about me, Alex? Could it be that my home looks like Swiss cheese by the hand of your men?"

"Hired mercenaries, no ties, no love lost. You realize this technology is considered critical warfare. Did you really think you were just going to march on in here with a handful of launchers and sell them off to these Neanderthals like the black market, creating chaos?"

"Be cautious with your tone, Alex," Dillon said. His voice did not quaver and his eyelids did not blink. He felt his jaw muscles pulse. "Tomorrow afternoon the world will know, and what I need is a name behind it, your name. The launchers I have painstakingly manufactured are not for sale. They are bait, per say. And they will reach the 'Neanderthal community' as you put it."

"You're delusional, Dillon. This..."

Dillon cut off his sentence. "After the demonstration, before any bidding, we will announce the merge of Maxwell and Portman together, side by side. I will then excuse myself and you will take over negotiations for future sales. The inventory is already being distributed."

"You're in over your head, Dillon. Yes, delusional is the word."

Dillon rapidly stood to his feet, knocking his chair back, and drew his nickel nine. Nerves jumped around the room like Mexican beans and men on both sides put their hands to their weapons in a combat-ready mode. Dillon turned the gun on its side, reflecting the fluorescent lighting in Alexander Portman's face as he placed it down on the table.

"I do not need to use fear tactics, Alex. This contract will speak for itself."

Patrick stepped forward and dropped a digital reader device on the table containing a copy of the merger contract. Alex defiantly pushed the reader across the table into Dillon's gun and backed up.

"I can tell you're not thinking straight at this time, Dillon," he said, "and you can't talk rationally with an irrational person. So I'm going to say goodnight now."

Alex turned to exit the room with his mind racing.

"Alex. Meet back here at eight tomorrow morning. Bring your attorney for the signing. This time will give you a chance to see more clearly."

Alex and his men cleared out of the Encore Room. He had no intention of making that meeting and every intention of stopping Dillon before he exposed the EL40. Tomorrow he would get his hands on the blueprints and eliminate the thorn, Dillon Maxwell.

*****

Lucy and I were on the dance floor holding on to our youth, while Don and John entertained Chris and her friends and followers. The Dutch Room was one of the many night clubs in the Hilton Towers. Don and John's choice for its saloon-like decor and cowgirl waitresses. John was putting on a show and Chris was falling for it.

"To hell with those mind gyms," he said. "We do it old school." He tried to show off his triceps by leaning on the table. "Ain't that right, Don?"

Don just rolled his eyes and let his brother look like an ass.

"Well, I require all our girls to do at least two sessions a week concentrating on abs," Chris said. "Some of the weapons they lift are extremely heavy and core strength is a necessity."

"I never thought about that," said Don, now showing interest.

"Kim, sweetie," Chris said. "Show them your abs."

She got up and raised her shirt a little too high on purpose. A little under-boob went a long way, clearly making her boss proud of the minor technique.

"With her core strength she can hold a weapon equal to her body weight steady and not even break a sweat," Chris stated with pride as John's Adam's apple echoed.

"Impressive," Don said.

*****

In a booth across the dance floor Jax and Grant ordered another round and sat in silence with wandering eyes, professional eyes that threw an unprofessional hitch at the sight of Kim's exposed flesh.

Kim lowered her shirt, rib by rib for effect, as Don's eyes shifted slightly, catching the two men awkwardly; fracturing their thoughts as if silently making a statement: *This is not your show, assholes*.

Jax and Grant shared a 'we got caught' look and both focused on the emblem at the bottom of their mugs for a second. Jax's eyes rolled to Lucy briefly as the mug came down. Then locked back on Grant, nodding ever so slightly.

*****

Alex and a couple of his closest men walked into the Pink Flamingo gentlemen's club and took seats in the middle of the establishment. With rotating chairs they could see three identical stages with catwalks and brass poles clad with flesh and lace. The girls knew not to approach Mr. Portman until invited, so they idled by and waited for the green light.

Cory sat on the end of the bar with elegance, legs exposed and crossed, sipping on a straw provocatively with ruby red lips. The spotlight hit her with flawless perfection as the DJ switched tracks and gave no introduction. All eyes were drawn to her milelong legs. She slowly uncrossed them, tantalizing just enough to get a rise. The beat of the music sped up following her motion as she high-stepped in six-inch heels to the stage. With agility and confidence she energized the room. She was all professional and knew how to lay the trap.

Gripping the pole with the back of her foot Cory climbed with effortless finesse. Twelve feet in the air she flipped her body upside down as the last piece of lace fell. With slight motion of a practiced foot against the boot-marked ceiling, the pole begin to spin, swirling a perfect display of goose pimpled flesh, firm and erect in all the right places. As her act came to a close she lay on her back, fully exposed, and grasped Alex with her transparent, green, lustful eyes… Ten minutes later she removed the cigar from his hands, took a seductive drag, knocked the cherry off in a ceramic flamingo and led him to a private room in the back.

The suite was plush with a full crystal-adorned bar, 1500 thread count Egyptian cotton linens and stimulating photography framed with a modern twist and authenticated by the National Gallery of Art. The main piece mounted over the bed was a black and white of a man and woman tangled in the throes of ecstasy. The signature at the bottom, in bold and beautiful calligraphy, read L.M. Grey.

Alex removed his gaze from the signature and Cory handed him a thick crystal glass containing a swig of bourbon.

"Here's looking at you, kid," she said and raised her glass for a toast.

Within minutes Cory was sitting on the corner of the bed, deep in thought. She looked over at Alex and gave his foot a flick. No response. "T'was the night before Christmas and all through the house," she whispered to herself as she set the glass down on the bar and knocked on the door to the adjacent room. Two men whom Cory had never seen before propped the door open and entered with a wheelchair. They removed Mr. Portman's limp body and shut the door behind them without so much as a hello.

"Not a creature was stirring, not even a mouse," she said and lowered herself back on silk sheets still warm from Portman's body. *Better than being cold*, she thought.

*****

Long time, Mr. Portman," Dillon said as Alex was brought in through the steel doors. "Let me introduce you to my good friends, Dr. Snyder and his lovely assistant Connie Lane."

Without any more words, the doctor and Connie got down to business. Dillon took his place in the chair alongside the inebriated Portman and allowed the doctor to work his magic, linking Dillon with Alex neurologically. It was over before he expected, and as the sensors were being removed all he could think of were dollar signs. With a permanent grin on Dillon's face he was removed to a recovery room and Alex was sent back to his lustful play date at the plush little cat house of The Flamingo. He would awaken with a slight headache and some physical fatigue from nothing more than an extensive roll with a beautiful goddess.

This was not the first time Dillon had been linked to another. He was actually born with a twin brother and over the years had developed a mind that could control and manipulate. With his brother the connection was strong. So strong, that out of pure anger Dillon had willed his sibling's brain to hemorrhage, with fatal results. The neuralinking was similar but the results were usually less intense. The ability to control the neural patterns came in more subtle and indirect ways, but nevertheless was obtainable.

Alexander Portman would make that meeting and sign the contract, giving Dillon $1.2 billion for the design and the technology of encapsulated energy. He would announce the merger of Maxwell and Portman Industries and would agree to the distribution of samples to over fifty of the largest arms dealers across the globe, ensuring future revenues.

# Chapter Nine

I woke up way too early after a fun-filled night of drinking and dancing. Don and John had won over the girls on the dance floor and Lucy got some great photos for memories. Last I could remember, Kim and Chris had dragged the boys back to their lair for some after-hours fun. The look on John's face was priceless.

"Good morning, sleepy head," Lucy said and handed me a fresh cup of Joe.

The smell was roasted and bold, just what I needed. It always amazed me how Lucy could bounce back from a late night of drinking. I just chalked it up to the fact that I consumed more than she.

"Where did you get this coffee?" I asked. "It's the crappy stuff from the bathroom counter."

"Great. Wait a minute, you're leaving aren't you?"

"Boy, I can't get away with anything, can I?"

"No siree, Bob. You know what I think? You're going to meet Chris for Bloody Marys and breakfast."

"We're staying in the building, don't worry. We are going to try that cute little bagel place, Tiffany's. I'll be back before you know it. Check on the boys. I hear they had quite a night. Being cooped up on a ship brings out the beast, I guess."

"That or whiskey shots and Yager bombs."

She kissed me goodbye, grabbed her camera and headed out the door like she was late.

"Bye, love," I shouted.

*****

The elevator doors slid open and Lucy snapped a picture capturing her image in the mirror-lined walls, smiled and started to hum a Vegas tune. She hit the lobby button and the close-door button simultaneously and hoped to bypass the middle floors. No such luck. A few floors down the polished doors opened to pick up riders. Two men stepped in and turned their backs to her without saying a word. She may have recognized them from the Dutch Room the night before, she thought, feeling a chill. Lucy hated fear but knew it was a part of life.

Still baffled that two well-dressed men in a five-star resort could cause uneasiness, she knew to not let her guard down. The hairs stood up on the back of her neck as she quickly played out a defense strategy in her mind. Faced with the speed and strength of her adversaries, she knew her efforts would be futile. *Step out, Lucy, step out.*

The brass doors came together, closing the option and confining her with the unknown. In the blink of an eye they turned. Two gloved hands grasped onto her throat, driving her to the back mirrored wall. Lucy brought her hands together, laced her fingers with a death grip and raised her arms straight up to the ceiling, breaking the man's grip. As the air returned to her lungs freely, her knee came up with all she had. The man's leg swept sideways, knocking her balance out. The other man wrapped his arms around her, lifting her off the floor and covering her mouth with a large gloved hand. She felt the prick of a needle in her right shoulder and both legs being lifted out from under her as the doors opened to another floor. Her phone and camera hit the floor as she faded. Lucy thought, *why didn't I scream? Everyone knows, the first thing you do is scream*, and the lights went out.

******

I spilled my coffee and did not know why. It was as if I nodded off. My focus was fuzzy as I rubbed my right shoulder. *What the hell*, I thought, and my mind flickered, *Lucy*. I immediately dialed her cell and it went straight to voice mail. I knew in my gut that something wasn't right. Frantically putting on my clothes, I called Don.

"What," he answered.

"Meet me downstairs now. I'll explain when I see you."

"Go back to sleep, Kenny. Besides, I'm not sure where I am."

"Goddamn it, Don. I told you guys to stay in the fucking building," I yelled. "Get over here. It's Lucy."

I bolted out the door and stopped in front of the elevators. *Which one, Lucy? Help me out, baby*. I drew my Ruger and held the sight on the doors to my right. I just had a feeling as the steel parted. Empty. I stepped in and while observing my surroundings, slipped the heat back in my shoulder rig, giving my arm a quick rub. I took note of the security cameras and thought of Lucy's Nikon. Kneeling down to the floor I spotted a small plastic piece wedged between the baseboard and the wall panel. As the elevator lowered I examined it. *A memory card - Lexar XQD SONY*. I placed it in my pocket and tried to clear my thoughts to make room for Lucy's. Strike out.

"Chris," I shouted as I came upon Tiffany's. "Where is she?"

Chris opened her eyes, reacting to my panic.

"I assume you're talking about Lucy. But she hasn't shown up yet. What's the problem?" she said.

I sat down hesitantly, put my elbows on the table and moved my hands as I spoke.

"Listen. I know she told you about the Neuralink."

"Yes, Ken, she told me."

"Well, I felt something, Chris. I know something bad has happened to her. And you sitting here alone is proof."

"That doesn't prove anything. She's a big girl, Ken. She can take care of herself, I'm sure."

I laced my fingers and pressed my thumbs to my temples.

"My thoughts aren't clear. It's like a drug, blurred."

"Have some water, Ken. Relax, I'm sure she will be here soon. Did you try calling her cell?"

I took a drink and almost spat it out.

"What do I look like, an idiot? Straight to voice mail."

"Don't get snippy with me, Ken. Let me try her again."

She got her phone out and noticed a text from Lucy saying that she was on her way. The time was 7:20 AM. She hit the callback button and one ring later, "You've reached Lucy. Leave me some love at the beep."

"Lucy. This is Chris. I'm here with Ken and you are freaking us out. Call me ASAP, hope everything is all right."

I looked Chris in the eyes with despair. She put her hand on my wrist.

"Give it a little time, sweetie, she'll call back," she said.

"I'm going to go check with security. See if they know anything."

"Good idea. Listen. I need to go report this morning for a couple of hours," she said. "Give me your number and I'll call you as soon as I'm free."

We exchanged numbers and hugged goodbye.

*****

Chris walked into the designated area for Portman Industries and could sense a buzz in the air. Kim spotted her and came up quick.

"Morning, Kim. So what time did you kick the McDreamies out?" she said.

They fell into step together, escorting each other to the prep room. Employees were moving 100 MPH, getting ready for the largest weapons demonstration known to man.

"They were still asleep when I left. Hey, did you hear something about a merge?"

"No, I just got here. Went to meet Lucy for breakfast but she never showed."

"Well, there's been some talk this morning. I heard the name Maxwell. I guess they're in negotiations as we speak."

"I've never even heard of Maxwell. That makes no sense at all. What line of industry is the merge?"

"I was hoping you could shed some light, nobody knows a thing. I guess Mr. Portman was acting strange this morning and someone heard him mumbling about a contract."

*****

The security booth for the Towers was just off the main entrance to an enormous casino engulfing the entire ground level. This was their main concern, the bread and butter of the operation. Explosions of light and sound invaded my senses as I approached the counter. Security Officer R.L. Sapien stood with his hands on his hips, immune to the sensory overload that I was experiencing.

"You're telling me she's gone? Is that correct?" he said after hearing my rant.

"Yes, she's gone. Have there been any reports at all, misconduct, anything? Do you have a database you can check?"

Sapien was small-framed with the aura of a man four times his size. His uniform was tightly pressed and creased, with a polished name plate and spit-shined boots you could see your reflection in. His skin was colored by artificial light which added to his intensity.

"Sir, you need to exit the floor. Go lie down for a while and think this through," he said.

"I need to see the security footage for the elevators in the north tower."

"I need you to pull your head out of your ass, clean the shit out of your ears and listen to me," he said sternly. "She's probably in the room next to yours getting railed by your best friend. Or she took your life savings to the roulette table over at the Tropicana.

Oh, no, you know what's even better? She hooked up with a multibillionaire and she's blowing him for chips right now. Go away, Mr. Detrick. On your own accord, before I have you removed in a most unsavory manner."

I gave him the Kraken death stare and suppressed my carnal instinct to rip his throat out.

"Thank you for your time, Sapien," I said.

I headed back towards the escalators going up to the lobby and called Don again. My eyes darted in all directions looking for Lucy even though I could feel nothing of her presence.

"Don. Where are you guys?" I said as soon as he picked up.

"Walking through the doors now, I was just going to call you."

"I'll tell you what, keep your eyes peeled for Lucy, I can't find her. I have a feeling she's left the building, and I mean against her will. I'll meet you at your room in ten minutes and we'll go from there. Load up."

"Will do."

I took the escalator three steps at a time and moved quickly through the lobby towards the north tower elevators. *Lucy, this isn't funny baby. Can you feel me? Give me a clue, something, anything*, I thought.

I took the same elevator up because I had a strange feeling that this was the last place we had connected. There was a smudged print on the mirror just above the chair rail. It looked like it could be from a woman's shoe. I ran my fingers over it and felt my heart jump.

*Be strong, Lucy.*

The door slammed hard against the stop and rattled the walls as I pushed through it, coming to a halt in the middle of our room. I did a quick look around then swung the closet doors open to load up. I slipped my Glock into the double shoulder holster, transferred my Ruger nine millimeter with fifteen round clip to the rig and put on my Danner boots, already equipped with two maxed out 15 round magazines up the side.

Like lightning I donned the shoulder rig, slung my shotgun and concealed my arsenal with a thick, tan duster handed down from my father. I felt like Django, the Western Warrior. Someone was going to pay.

*Here comes the tax man, motherfuckers.*

"Holy crap, Ken. Did the defecation hit the oscillator?" John said as I let the door crash closed behind me.

"No time for jokes, jackass. Load up and load heavy, we got to go."

"Slow down, Ken. We've got to use our brains before brawn, buddy," Don said. "Fill us in here, we're kind of in the dark."

I took a breath to calm my nerves and spoke slowly, fighting the moisture that pressured my tear ducts.

"Lucy is gone."

"Okay, we've got that part. How do you know she didn't just run down for some chocolate or something?"

"I felt it. She didn't answer her phone, she didn't meet with Chris like she said she was... She's gone, guys... Vanished."

"What do you mean, you felt it?"

"I got dizzy, felt fear, distress, confusion, all at the same time. I spilled my coffee for Christ's sake. I think I'm going to be sick."

"Sit down for a minute, bro. Have a drink," John said. He poured some cheap Canadian whiskey he had picked up at the gift shop and handed me a glass.

Don put two and two together.

"You must have Neuralinked with Lucy. How come you didn't tell us?" he said.

"Because we knew how you would react. That's beside the point. The issue now is that Lucy is gone and I feel no connection to her whatsoever. It's as if we're no longer linked."

"That's probably temporary. It means she's been knocked out or drugged up to slow her brain activity. John and I have both experienced that feeling of disconnect."

"That doesn't make me feel any better. The elevator is the key. That's where they took her, I know it. We need to get the surveillance footage and time is ticking."

"Well, let's go ask, I don't think it will be a problem."

"I tried that. I spoke to the head guy on the floor, a real prick, something L. Sapien. The guy's got little man's syndrome bad, wouldn't budge. So I'm going to stick this shotgun in his mouth and see if his attitude changes."

"You're gonna get us all killed like that, Ken. There's got to be a better way," Don said.

My phone rang and I picked up fast without checking the caller I.D.

"Lucy?"

"I take it you haven't heard from her?" Chris said.

"Chris? No, nothing. I didn't expect you to call so soon."

"I didn't expect to either. I'm covered for now though, but I need to be back for the show. What can I do, Ken? I feel like I need to do something."

"I don't know, I'm not thinking straight… First thing we're going to do is get our hands on the security footage from that elevator, though. They're not wanting to cooperate so it might get ugly."

"Ken, that doesn't sound good. Who did you talk to?"

"Some little Mexican Barney Fife named Sapien."

"Don't do anything stupid. These guys don't mess around, Ken. Let me make some phone calls first. I'll pull the contact list for the Towers, they're clients of ours, see what I can do. Which elevators?"

"North tower, between seven and eight this morning."

"I'm on my way. Just stay put. What room are you in?"
"Seven fourteen, how long are you going to be? We're ready to go, Chris."

"Give me fifteen. Don't move."

The phone went dead and I looked over at John.

"Pour me another, bro. It's going to be a minute," I said.

Chris showed up exactly fifteen minutes after she terminated our call. I paced the entire time like a caged lion waiting for his scraps.

"Any luck?" I asked her before she had crossed the threshold.

"There is no footage, Ken, and no explanation other than technical difficulties. Everything on that leg, even the floor cams, malfunctioned for about a twenty-minute window. Enough time for them to clear out completely."

I shattered my glass into the mirror wall behind the desk.

"That's bullshit," I shouted in frustration. "Let's go."

I headed for the door and Chris grabbed my arm with the strength of a man.

"Ken. Stop it. Blowing up the Hilton Towers is not going to bring her back. Now sit down and let's think this through," she commanded.

I looked at Chris, relaxed my shoulders a bit and exhaled through my nostrils.

"Have a seat, Ken," Don said as he moved his bulk to block the doorway.

I swiveled a chair, sat with my back against the wall and looked at the ceiling. I had to close my eyes to keep the room from spinning. My frontal lobe began to pulse slightly like I was just about to leave the world of the awake and enter slumber. Blinking a couple of times and moving my head from side to side I started to mumble.

"Help... Ken... camera."

"What did you say?" Don asked.

"Help... Ken... camera."

"I think he's connecting again," John said.

"Where is Lucy's camera?" Chris asked.

*****

Lucy opened her eyes and was looking at the back of a man leaning over a counter. The light was bright white fluorescent, shining off the back of his full head of hair. She thought she recognized him but needed to see his face to be sure.

"Dr. Snyder?" she asked.

He looked over his shoulder, briefly revealing himself, then back down at his work without saying a word as Dillon stepped through the steel doors to the mobile unit.

"Do you two know each other?" he asked.

Lucy's eyes did not blink and her lips felt like they were glued shut, rendering her speechless, and Dr. Snyder just ignored the question.

Dillon reached over Dr. Snyder's arm and picked Lucy's I.D. up off the counter.

"Lucy Marie Grey," he read aloud. "What a beautiful name, a familiar one at that. Five foot seven, one hundred and twenty pounds, blond hair, blue eyes. Oooo-eeee, lips of an angel."

He bent down and put his face in front of Lucy's.

"Let me see that tongue, baby. Can you touch your nose?" he asked.

Lucy went to slap his face with disgust and realized that her arms were bound to the chair. She shook violently from side to side and opened her mouth to scream but Dr. Snyder was behind her. He inserted a black shiny ball gag, slightly under the size of an eight ball, and buckled the straps firmly behind her head. Her jaw felt like it was about to snap.

"Let's get this over with. I've got to get this idiot out of my mind," Dillon said and took a seat next to Lucy.

Connie came into the room and glanced at Lucy. Her eyes immediately went to Dr. Snyder. They shared an intense look, and then quickly went to work prepping their patients. Thirty minutes later, Lucy succumbed to a nightmare. *****

"Ken. Wake up," Don yelled.

He was gripping my cheeks, pressing into my teeth as I nodded. I could hear him but was unable to respond verbally. I was n a state of shock; fatigue was taking over as I felt Lucy slip away. My world was crashing, hit with depression, nausea, a punch to the liver, chest pains, and an uppercut from Iron Mike. My brain was scrambled. *Lucy, I love you, I'm sorry...* And the lights went out.

*****

Dillon felt like a new man. He couldn't wait to finish up his business and hit the skyway. He had thought of linking with one of his victims in the past but had never gone through with it. This was going to be the ultimate treat, a feast for royalty. He would experience every tear, every whimper, and every plea. All her childhood fears would manifest through the flesh of his hand and the darkness of his own soul. He would reap the benefits through mind and body.

"Enriquez, this one is special. Take good care of her. Not a scratch, understood?" Dillon said.

Enriquez acknowledged, feeling Dillon's command in his marrow.

"Not a scratch, yes sir. She's in good hands."

Two men entered the room and removed Lucy from the recovery table. They carried her out through the steel doors like she was a bag of trout chow from the feed depot, not a worry in the world. They laid her down in the cargo hold of a small hovercraft and secured the hatch. Enriquez nodded his head, strapped in and set course for The Claiborne with Dillon's precious prey.

*****

I slowly opened, then closed my eyes, not sure if I was ready to face reality. Lucy had disconnected for good this time. I could hear Chris on her phone. She was asking questions and I could tell was getting nowhere.

"How long was I out?" I asked, blinking to focus.

"A couple of hours. Don and John are out talking to some staff to see what they can come up with," she said. "Hey, where is Lucy's camera? You said something about a camera just before you passed out."

"She took it with her. I remember her having it when she left. Oh yeah," I said like a light switched on in my head. "I found this in the elevator."

I took the memory card from my pocket and held it out for Chris.

"What the hell, Ken? What's on it?"

"I don't know. I don't think it's hers. It says Lexar Sony on it. Lucy has a Nikon."

"You idiot. It's probably compatible with Nikon. Let me see it."

She took the card out of my hand, inserted it into her netpad and had the images up within seconds.

"It's hers, all right," she said.

I quickly moved behind her to view.

"Project them up," I snapped.
The photos appeared over the net-pad and Chris scrolled slowly by swiping her hand through the projected screen. The first images were from the club the night before, with some hallway shots heading back to the room followed by some of me undressing. Next was a close-up of the crappy coffee pot in our bathroom, then one of Lucy's reflection.

"Stop," I said on the next image.

"It looks like a boot," Chris said.

It was a dark leather boot with some kind of rusted rivets and thick stitching. I stared at it for a minute.

"Okay."

The boot switched and we were looking at an up-shot of the back of two men, nothing distinguishing.

"Next," I said.

I squinted my eyes as the face appeared. The photo was a little blurry, as if he was rapidly turning and the action mode was not set on the camera.

"Can you focus that?" I asked.

"A little, I'll give it a shot," Chris said as Don and John walked in.

"No luck. Nobody knows shit," John said in frustration. "What's this?"

"Lucy snapped off some shots of these assholes and dropped the memory card or it fell out when her camera hit the floor," I explained.

"No way, that's Lucy for ya," Don said. "Way to go."

Chris got the last photo to clear up a bit. One man still had his back to Lucy with a partial fuzzy face in the mirror's reflection, but the other, turning in a lunging motion, was much more distinguishable. I figured that Lucy must have been shooting from the hip and probably didn't have a prayer of defending herself.

"I've seen that guy," John blurted out. "He was at the fights. Yeah, I'm sure of it, he was standing behind Mr. Portman when that creepy guy was talking to him, remember?"

"You know what? I think that guy was at the club last night," Don said.

I studied the face, burning him into my brain.

"I think that guy talking to Alex has something to do with the merge," Chris said.

"What merge? What are you talking about?" I asked.

Chris explained what she had heard and how something wasn't right.

"Alex would never have done this, they must have leverage of some kind," she said. "They're going to announce it at the demo. Maxwell, I think. I'm sure this guy is connected with Maxwell."

"Well, let's go check this guy out. I'll put this to his dick," I said, raising my shotgun. "Get some answers real quick."

# Chapter Ten

    The transportation centers were packed with people. It took us over an hour to get out to the weapons demonstration grounds. Thousands of acres, desert as far as the eye could see, with the main lights of Vegas glowing like a never ending background sunset, despite the time of day. This was clearly a military test site, well organized for control, separating the spectators from friendly fire and securing the sky to a certain altitude, keeping boneheads from being in the wrong place at the right time to lose their lives. There were many forums for different weapon demonstrations. Luckily Chris knew exactly where to go for Portman Industries.

    The ground was wet and muddy, caking our boots as we walked the maze. They must have showered the terrain. Better than chewing every breath, I suppose. Gunfire was breaking the sound barrier and cracking off every hard surface it could reach. Nerves couldn't help but jump with adrenaline. We could also hear explosions, ooh's and aah's, and if you listened real close through the chaos of the war zone, you could make out the sound of money changing hands. Ear plugs and brochures were given out at each gate. They were a must.

Thirty minutes later we arrived at a massive area on the outskirts, where most of the aerial work would be demonstrated. MPs were at the entrance checking passes. Chris flashed hers and stepped past the gates. The MP put a hand up, stopping my movement to follow.

"Sorry, boys, you'll have to go around the side. That's the entrance for general spectators," he stated and gave a full arm point in that direction.

"They're with Portman, officer," Chris said. "They're addons."

"No on list, no on entry," he stated with finality. "They can access Mr. Portman's spectator box and wait for you there." This additional information was offered way above and beyond his line of duty and clearly should have been taken as such.

Chris looked at us and shrugged her shoulders.

"Go hang out in the box and I'll call you in a few," she said and gave us an apologetic look.

Portman's sky-box was a penthouse, four stories up the I-beam framed box-like structure. It was a spacious panoramic viewing room which I could only assume was wrapped with bulletproof, floor to ceiling, transparent acrylic. Images of beautiful women wearing next to nothing were cast like ghosts caught in the acrylic. They paced the room showing off a variety of weapons, closing the actions, sighting, slinging, and blowing imaginary smoke proactively from barrels.

"Hey. That's Kim right there," Don said, recognizing her curves. It was amazing how facial recognition was not required.

It was as if she had heard him, because with perfect timing she looked our way and blew a kiss.

I looked through her semi-transparent figure down to a platform stage with an enormous digital monitor as a backdrop. I spotted Chris with a few of the live models on one end of the stage. No sign of Alex Portman or the man in the photo. The girls were cast on the monitor as they walked along the edge, bending over to interact with the crowd and potential buyers, hugging, kissing cheeks, posing for snapshots and signing autographs. They were celebrities to these drooling gun freaks. Chris made her way to the back of the stage and engaged in conversation with a man. I focused my sight on Alex Portman.

Alex moved to a rise in the middle of the platform and began to narrate by heart with extraordinary control. The tone of his voice commanded attention. He started off with a little history lesson on the evolution of warfare while enthusiasts and fans hung on his every word.

My phone buzzed and broke the trance of the anti-Christ.

"Ken. It's Chris. Alex said he'll meet with you." "Any sign of our mystery man?" I asked.

"Not yet. Alex said something happened last night with this Maxwell guy but didn't elaborate much, said he's a real sicko."

"Seems strange that he's willing to meet so fast. What did you tell him?"

"Just that we needed to know what happened. That it was a matter of life and death. He said box twenty-three after the demo. I'll bring him up, got to go."

Chris disconnected and I looked at Don.

"Waiting on Chris again. This guy is spooked or something. Hand me your eyes," I said, holding my hand out to Don .I scanned the faces with Don's high powered binoculars as I filled him in.

"No sign of this prick," I said to no one in particular.

"He's got to be here," Don said.

Alex pointed to the sky, temporarily blinding the audience with pyrotechnics as if they were fired out of his fingertips with the will of his mind. A large hovercraft rose from behind the stage as our eyes refocused. Alex's voice thundered with excitement as he explained the electrical current creating the magnetic field formed before us. An audible gasp was heard as the craft was struck and the body shuddered as if it was incurring severe turbulence. The drone plummeted to the ground in the distance and the monitor filled with fire as it exploded on impact. A Ducati glider equipped for combat swung into view, hovering above the stage. A retracting arm swiveled the smoking EL40, returning it to its seated position.

The crowd was in awe… Utterly speechless.

Dillon disconnected his oxygen lines, removed his helmet and set the glider down on the stage to thunderous applause. Alex gave him an introduction fit for a king. Jax and Grant entered the stage and Jax stripped the microphone from Alex rather aggressively.

"The EL40 is the future," he exclaimed. "One hundred percent mobile."

Grant held a launcher above his head as the cameras zoomed in and filled the screen with a close up of the EL40 as a small hovercraft drone rocketed at high speed over the stage, creating a powerful energy field. Ray was lying in wait, positioned on the corner of the platform with his thumbs on the butterfly trigger spade handle of a fifty caliber machine gun. The fifty-cal was mounted solid on an M3-tripod and could deliver 750 to 850 rounds per minute. Ray depressed and held, lighting up the craft with no damaging effect. It was nothing but a pretty light show, displaying the power of a high speed magnetic force. The drone made another pass and Grant quickly dropped to one knee, brought the handheld launcher into position, locked the site on his target and depressed the trigger pad. The impact was caught perfectly on the viewing screen before our eyes. The drone weaved out of control as Ray loaded it up with standard fifty caliber rounds, shredding it to parmesan before it had a chance to drop altitude.

The timing was impeccable and the masses loved it.

"These guys are fucking badass," John said to no one in particular.

"That's them, Ken," Don said, ignoring John's comment. "How do you suppose we get to them?"

"The guy holding the launcher is definitely the one that took Lucy," I said. "I don't know what's up with all this macho gun shit and merge, whatever, or how we're going to get to him. But right now Portman is our only link to these guys. So he's gonna talk."

None of the spectators in the box knew of Maxwell and they were floored by the demonstration of the EL40, casting confusion on the whole situation. There was no way to get down and gain access right now, and every second felt like an eternity knowing Lucy's captors were within sight. I paced the back of the viewing box like a gladiator in wait and listened to a rehearsed explanation of the merge with Maxwell Industries by Portman himself.

After several minutes of scrambled thought I rang Chris.

"You need to get out of there as soon as possible. I have a bad feeling about all of this. I don't think you should ask any more questions about these guys, either. You should have never gone in there, Chris. Just grab Portman and get up here, let me do the talking."

"I'll get there as soon as I can, Ken. It's a freakin' zoo down here," she replied.

*****

The Claiborne was a massive vessel, a three-hundred-foot mega yacht made by the Dutch for pure luxury and stature. Originally The Claiborne was maintained by a twenty-five-person crew, 24-7, 365 days a year. Now, she was ignored 365 days a year by three overpaid middle age wops from Queens, New York. All they were required to do was have The Claiborne in the right place at the right time -- Dillon's time. Sitting off the coast of Fort Lauderdale, Florida, they eagerly awaited a package for their boss en route from Las Vegas.

Tony's phone rang; the man in charge while Dillon was away.

"Coming in, is the pad clear on the main deck? Let's get her straight to the suite, she's a feisty one," Enriquez said.

"All clear, bring her home," Tony responded.

The Claiborne was anchored far enough off the coastline to be out of sight of land-goers, and from its decks, only white caps from a rough Atlantic surface could be seen, no matter the direction. The wind was howling and visibility was poor. Tony sighted through the scope to the north while his co-crew tended to other matters. Enriquez came into view like a speck of pepper on dark grey cotton.

Lucy could hear Enriquez talking and started kicking her legs against the side of the craft, then thought better of it. She should save her energy for what lies ahead.

"Turn the guide on, asshole. I can't see shit out here," Enriquez snapped.

"Use your GPS," Tony shot back.

"How do you think I found you? Connection is in and out with the weather."

Tony ran to the control panel to activate the ship's laser guided landing assist system. He targeted the dot in the sky and hit the lock-on button. A beam of light shot out of a porthole in the center of the main deck's landing pad and connected with the hovercraft, illuminating the magnetic field with a red hue. Enriquez felt the guide system engage and relaxed for the pull.

"You're set, Enriquez, see you in a few," Tony said.

Tony watched the wet, salty air trickle through the light of the beam from the overcast sky above. The clouds were getting darker and the swell of the ocean just a little more agitated.

The guide system worked like a charm and pulled Enriquez to the platform with finesse. The men exchanged meaningless greetings and popped the cargo hatch.

Lucy's mind was struggling with an intruder, erasing what little clarity she had regained. Images of violence and destruction strangled thoughts of family and friends... *Ken, I need you...* A small child was being burned with the butt of a cigarette, pleading with helpless cries, a glass of clear liquid shattered on the dirty concrete floor at a woman's bare feet with shards of glass penetrating her ankles... *Ken, help me...* She felt her mother's loving embrace one second, then the brief comfort was stripped away violently by the hot breath of an enraged father snarling inches from her face with glowing eyes and large teeth tarnished by neglect and potted with tobacco. All Lucy could do was shake her head and grind her teeth in agony and confusion.

Tony and Enriquez grabbed her with the speed of a cobra, snapping her out of the trance. Her muscles convulsed as she jerked her body, trying to slip their grip. Realizing that she was still bound at the wrists and ankles, she screamed a muffled cry and tasted duct tape between her lips. *Oh, please God, help me.* Tears ran from her eyes and nose, aiding the rain in soaking the teak wood deck as she tried to resist the strength of the men.

"You're gonna settle down, bitch. Or I'll give you something to cry about," Tony said, tightening his grip and pushing his arms against her chest.

Lucy vaguely recalled Dillon saying that she wasn't to be touched, but she decided not to test them any longer, not knowing how deep their loyalty ran. They carried her to Dillon's suite and pushed her to the tile floor in the lavish expanse of the master bath. She was face down over the threshold of a solid steel door leading off to a small, square concrete room containing a roll of 2-ply, a bottle of water and a toilet. Lucy pushed up on all fours to protest but Tony put a boot on her tailbone and shoved her through the doorway, driving her head first into the toilet. She rolled into a fetal position, head pounding, intensified by the harsh smell of bleach and tried to clear her mind of the penetrating foreign images.

"We'll be back in a minute, get comfy," Tony said and slammed the cell door, throwing the bolt and leaving Lucy to nothing but her infected thoughts. Infected like a mad virus.

"She is smoking," Tony said.

Enriquez slapped him on the back of the head as they walked.

"You idiot. Dillon said she's not to be touched. If he sees any marks on her I'm pointing the finger at you, fuck face."

"Well, I ain't putting up with no shit. She better stay in line."

"Just let me handle this one," Enriquez said. "Let's get a drink and look at those mounts."

It was starting to get very wet out and Enriquez was tired from the trip, but he knew that Dillon would not be far behind. So the launchers would be mounted and operational, and Lucy would be prepped appropriately for his arrival.

"Where are those two Guidos you hang out with?" Enriquez asked.

"They're down on the lower deck making the rounds."
"Well, get them up here and make sure they know Lucy is off limits."

They knocked back their shots of whiskey to warm the body and donned some slickers to fight the elements of the growing storm and got to work. Enriquez knew Dillon would be pleased with the mounts. Specs were spot-on and the modification to dual paddle triggers was the cherry on top. He laid the mobsters out on the first unit so it was done right and left the second one in their hands, crossing his fingers.

"Let me know when you're done," Enriquez said.

He motioned for Tony to follow him back to the main deck. They went through the slider to the suite and forced the door shut amidst the pressure and the ocean rain. Shaking off their drenched slickers, Enriquez toweled his face and poured another round of whiskey.

"I'm gonna need you to stay out here, Tony. Just keep an ear out. If I need you I'll let you know, okay?"

"I guess," he said with a bummed tone, obviously wanting to get a little more action on Lucy.

They both took their shots and Tony poured another as Enriquez went to deal with Lucy.

*****

We ran down the corridor to find box twenty-three. It was all the way at the end past several other private viewing rooms. Each room had a different set of personal security standing watch. I wondered what kind of salary would make a man throw himself in harm's way for another. I was glad to have Don and John on my side. It made me think of the worth of friendship.

"You can wait here, Mr. Detrick," a large concrete figure said as we approached the section containing boxes twenty-two through twenty-six. "Mr. Portman is on his way."

I nodded my head to say okay and looked around. I felt a little uncomfortable as I did not see any chairs or waiting area to accommodate us. So we stood awkwardly against the wall with the other concrete security staff of the unknown. I crossed my arms and looked up and down the hall as I whistled softly the '*Do not laugh when the hearse goes by*' tune my father used to sing to me as a child. It was supposed to help with patience. My mood was dark and my patience just wore further. I think my neck started to twitch.

"What the hell, Guss? I told you to let them in," Alex yelled as he and Chris spotted us waiting.

"I thought you said don't let them in, sir," Guss responded with a stutter.

"I don't want people seeing them out here. Use your brains. Chop, chop," Alex said and motioned towards the door.

There was no doubt in my mind that if Guss had let us in and had been instructed not to, he would have suffered a much harsher consequence than a tongue lashing. We followed Alex into the plush private sky box like little ducklings. Guss shut the door behind us and assumed his post as a dutiful roadblock outside the door.

"Have a seat, gentlemen," Alex said. "Chris, could you tend the bar please? I need a vodka and tonic."

John kicked the bar stool out from under Alex as he was in motion to sit. Alex's ass hit the floor hard, casting a look of disbelief and pain across his pompous face. Before he could react further John had him by the throat and dragged him to a white leather swivel chair, planting him with utter ease. As John released his grip, Alex's vocals began to produce. His half squeak was muffled by a snapping blow to his windpipe from the web of John's hand.

"We are not here to drink, Alex. And if you try to alert your man at the door you will be dead before he enters the room. Are we clear?" I said as I took the opposing leather seat.

My eyes were glued on Alex as he nodded compliance.

"Now," I continued, "Let me get to the point. Your little friends down there that just put on a show for us all are going to die soon. You may or may not be subjected to the same fate depending upon your answers. It appears to me that by you joining forces with Maxwell, you know of their doings."

"I don't... I don't... I'm on your side here. You have to trust me," he sputtered.

Alex was clearly distraught, but in a state of escalating panic, sweating as he tried to come to terms with his predicament. "Do not stutter, Alex. Slow down and measure your words. They might be your last."

"I don't know what happened," he said. "I want to help. Do you think I would have agreed to see you guys alone in my private box if I didn't want to help?"

"Help with what? Do you know why we are here, Alex?"

"Chris said it was a matter of life and death." He shook his head as if clearing foggy thoughts. "Dillon fucked with my mind. I don't know how, but he did. I'm turned upside down, man."

"Quit being a basket, Alex. Calm down. Chris, go ahead and give him some courage. Vodka, was it?"

He nodded and swallowed dry as his eyes glossed over.

"Now who is Dillon?" I asked, snapping my fingers towards Chris for the beverage. I knew he was ready to break. Either this guy was a real wimp or a hell of an actor.

"Dillon Maxwell. This guy's a real freak. Somehow he put his thoughts in my head. Dark thoughts. Like nightmares. He was driving me mad from the inside. Controlling. A puppeteer of illusions. But it was more than that. I couldn't tell what was real, real thoughts, my thoughts, his. I was literally on the verge of taking my own life last night… Then poof. He was gone."

"Okay… I want to know who he is… exactly. Where's he from, what's he do, Alex?"

"He's a killer is what he is. I've seen it. You have to stop him, Ken. Before he kills again. Before he kills your Lucy."

I blinked back agitation.

"I never mentioned Lucy, Alex." I rose to my feet slowly, waiting for a response before I took this to the next level.

Alex shook his head and stuttered on.

"Chris told me who you guys are and told me about Lucy. I think I saw her. I saw her with Dillon."

I looked at Chris as she came around the bar and handed the vodka to Alex. She gave me a quizzical, 'I'm sorry' expression. I sat down and buried my eyes in my right hand for a moment, massaging my temples, then stared at Alex as he downed the vodka, waiting for my response.

"What did you see?"

"It was like a dream, obscure, yet real. Twisted shit. Can't remember all of it but when Chris told me her name I recalled I had heard that name. As if it was being read off an I.D. or driver's license. Lucy Marie Grey. Then a woman's face flashed… her face… with tears streaming down her checks. She had cords or wires on her head and a woman standing behind her. Then Dillon's face appeared in front of hers as if he was going to kiss her. It was as if, in that image, he was saying 'watch me rape, body and mind.' A terror washed over me, gripping my insides. The vision blinked to a sink with water running crimson to a brass drain. He was washing life blood from his homicidal hands."

Alex stopped talking and just stared into the distance.

"Wires. You know what it sounds like, Ken," Don said, "Neuralink. This guy linked with Alex here, then with Lucy. That's why you both lost connection around the same time, he's mind jumping."

"Where's he heading, Alex? How do I get to him?" I asked with frustration, imagining Lucy's turmoil.

"I don't know."

"If you're not being straight with me, Alex…"

"I don't know. He's like a ghost. All I did was sign a contract buying into production and distribution of the energy launcher, but the funds went to offshore accounts, no address, no contact numbers," he said.

"What else do you remember? You said you saw him kill."

"Nightmares… Images of blood and flesh. He talks to them. Gets them to react just before…"

"Before what? How does he kill them? I need to know, Alex. Everything you've got."

Alex's eyes looked at me, full of water and fear. I could tell he genuinely did not want to continue. He diverted his gaze and began to speak in a much softer tone. Barely audible.

"He rapes, Ken. Cuts, bludgeons, strangles, bleeds them out for the scent of iron… The scent is what he wants… It's like perfume to him, Ken. The most potent and distinguishable kind."

"That's enough," Don said, stopping his rant that was clearly going to continue. "This is not helping, Ken. We need to get down to that Neuralink exhibit and see what we can come up with."

Don was just trying to keep me focused. We all knew this was going nowhere but this testimony was like a train wreck. Alex was in pieces and re-experiencing the trauma was cluttering his thoughts. I pressed the last question with my tone.

"Alex. Where do you think he would go? Where do you think he would take Lucy?" I asked.

"I don't know. The only reoccurring image I have is of a small boat out in choppy water. A fishing boat, I think. He must be fond of water."

*****

Lucy was feeling nauseous from the motion of The Claiborne, the institutional concrete of her cold cell and the fear of what lay ahead. Her chest was convulsing as her anger grew, causing her to hyperventilate. She buried her head in the steel toilet and dry heaved, bruising her abs from within, twisting her insides, retching every drop of disdain she could muster.

"Do I need to come back? Or are you done?" Enriquez said from the doorway, looking Lucy over with wondering eyes.

The light poured in from around his silhouette, making him appear much larger and more physically dominant than reality. Lucy rolled to her buttocks and put her head back against the wall, staring daggers into the shadow.

"Time to clean up, little senorita," Enriquez said and threw a thin cotton football jersey to the floor by her feet. It was light grey with double zeros on the front and back. "Scrub up well and wash your hair. You've got fifteen minutes, young lady, and expect the white glove."

He reached down and removed the bindings from her ankles and wrists, stepped back through the door and took a seat on the marble counter topping the dual vanity.

Lucy slowly got to her feet, rubbing her wrists to circulate blood, peeked through the door and surveyed her surroundings. The shower door was transparent but spotted with calcium. A corner tub was lined with porthole windows displaying the vastness of the ocean and sending her into a submissive state. Mirrors decorated the walls with brass anchors inlayed around their perimeters. Streak marks from poor cleaning showed on all surfaces. The toilet was unattended with a wooden tank mounted high on the wall donning the word Claiborne in brass letters. A patina pull chain dangled from the underside. Few supplies had been left on the counter -- next to Enriquez and his wondering eyes -- for her prep work and there was no doubt in her mind that the rest of the room had been stripped of goods. With an old towel on the toilet, this is what she had to work with.

"A little privacy, please?" she said.

"Clock's ticking," Enriquez responded and held her stare while he dug at his teeth with a wooden toothpick.

Realizing that he had no intention of moving she took a seat on the edge of the soaker tub.

"You either get in that shower, or I'm going to put you there. And you won't like my methods," Enriquez said with malice.

He pulled an eight-inch serrated Ka-Bar with a carbon handle from his boot sleeve, examined his teeth and gums in the shiny reflection of the blade and re-sheathed.

Lucy got the point, put the cotton jersey and the towel on the hook by the shower and stepped inside.

"Leave the bra and panties," Enriquez instructed.

Lucy blew air out between her teeth in disgust but threw the items over the glass doors to the floor. The water warmed up quick and felt good on her muscles. She did not look at Enriquez, keeping her back towards him, not wanting to give him the pleasure. She steamed up the door as much as possible and stayed under the water until he instructed her to get out.

"Times up, comb through your hair good and pull it back in a ponytail," he said after about 10 minutes.

Felt like two to Lucy but it was actually a well needed two minutes. All she could think about as she turned the water off was jamming that blade deep in this guy's gut. She had to make a move soon but the time was not right. She pulled the towel and shirt in, dried off a bit and put the shirt on. Her body was slightly wet and the cotton stuck to her curves a little too much for comfort. She pulled down on the shirt, stretching the fabric to cover her privates and in doing so exposed cleavage.

"This is ridiculous, can I have my bra and panties, please?" she pleaded.

"Get out."

She closed her eyes and took a deep breath, held it and exhaled through her anger-flared nostrils. *Courage, Lucy.* As she exited the shower, images flashed in her mind and weakened her at the knees, bringing her down. Enriquez caught her and propped her up on the worn toilet seat.

"Don't fuck around, Lucy," he snapped, already holding the blade in front of her face. He raised and lowered the sharp, polished steel, flickering movie frames in the wet of her eyes, spitting blood and foam at her like a rabid dog crossing into the red zone.

"Don't, don't, don't," she screamed, begging for the nightmare to stop.

Enriquez dragged the crimson-covered blade slowly across his tongue inches from her face so she could see the blood in his mouth.

She closed her eyes hard, bringing her cheeks to her eyebrows, but the image remained burned to her lids with a rainbow of colors, failing at concealment.

Enriquez was holding a glass of water to her lips trying to calm her down and pull her from the destructive, hallucinatory trance. After all, it was his job to preserve this young thing.

"Breathe, Lucy, come on, take a drink," he said.

She opened her eyes, locking on his gaze, and put both hands around the glass to drink. With the coordination and instinct of a crazed killer she sprung to her feet, planting them firmly on the toilet seat and came down hard and fast with both hands, driving the base of the thick bar-glass into the top of her victim's head. The glass shattered in her hands, splitting his scalp open as he dropped to the floor. Consumed with bloodthirst, she hammered her knee down onto his manhood, slipped the knife from his boot and drove the blade up into his chin towards the brain. She saw the life drain from his eyes and noticed the tip of the Ka-Bar extruding from the top of his split skull. Her hands were tightly fastened to the carbon handle. It took effort to release her grip. The door flew open and by an unknown instinct, Lucy slipped the Glock from Enriquez's shoulder holster and pumped two rounds into Tony's chest before he could register the scene. His body flew back, crashing over a chair to a white tabletop, sliding off the side and leaving a thick smear of bold red over the bright marble surface.

Lucy knew her time was limited. The shots were bound to be heard and she had no idea who was in earshot. The tap water burned over her palms as she rinsed the blood from her hands, watching red tears drip to the drain. As pain registered she realized shards of crystal would need to be removed from the web of her right hand and the love-and life-lines of her left. Using an old army knife she found on Tony, she gritted her teeth and cleared the fragments, wrapping her hands with strips of towel. She did a quick rinse on the gun, slipped her shoes on and fled the suite as fast as possible.

*****

Dillon had cleared Las Vegas with efficiency considering the congestion of crafts. He was a very wealthy man who had Portman right where he wanted him. He had directed some of his crew back to the Sedona shop instead of cluttering The Claiborne. After all, this was a time for celebration and relaxation. His usual men would suffice in keeping the defenses up for this trip. Experiencing an adrenaline level spike, Dillon felt needles prick his hands like they were falling asleep. For a second he thought heart attack. Then remembered his lovely Lucy and dialed Enriquez for an update.

"Something's not right," he said to Jax. "Get Tony on the line."

"He's not picking up?" Jax questioned.

"No, he's not picking up. Now get Tony."

"Relax, I'm sure everything's okay," Jax said as he dialed.

"Goddamn it. Pick up. I told them not to mess with her. I swear Jax, if they lay one finger on her."

"Went to voice mail, boss."
Enriquez's line finally picked up.

"Yellow," a voice said in a somber tone. And it was not the voice of the phone's owner.

"I assume you have a good explanation for answering this line," Dillon snapped.

"Is the fact that he is dead good enough?" the voice replied.
Dillon could barely contain his fury.

"Is this Joe? Where's the girl, Joe?" Dillon said.

"She's gone, Dillon. There's blood everywhere. I don't know what the fuck happened. I heard a gun pop twice, ran in and picked up the line. Swear to God."

"You're going to swear to me, Joe. Put me on cam and show me Enriquez."

Joe fiddled with the phone for a second and pointed the cam at the scene. Dillon slid his phone device into a dock in the console and the video image appeared on the monitor. Joe scanned the bathroom, coming to a halt on Enriquez's face. The knife was embedded through his head and his eyes were open like they froze at the sight of a ghost. Brown marbles peering through pools of fresh plasma.

"Yeah, he looks dead all right," Dillon said.

Joe panned the phone cam over to Tony's corpse so they didn't have to ask about him.

"Holy shit," said Jax.

"Are those your footprints in the blood, Joe?" Dillon asked.

"No, sir. They lead out to the main deck but it's wet out, so I doubt they go far. They are small so I'm guessing they're your girl's."

"Find her, goddamn it. It's a ship. She can't go far," Dillon ordered.

He disconnected with Joe in disgust and phoned Grant, who should have been in Sedona by this time.

"Grant... Dillon... Change of plans. Send a team down to The Claiborne now, we've got a runner. Jax will send you the coordinates. I want you to stay put there though, okay? Keep some guys with you and lock it down tight. I don't need any more headaches. You got that? No headaches, Grant."

"Got it, boss, no worries."

Grant did what he was instructed to but it made him sick to hear himself kiss ass. *Yes, boss, no worries, boss,* he repeated in his head. He would hide out like a rabbit in his hole, protecting Dillon's precious trash. And every minute would bring his ulcer one step closer to rupture.

# Chapter Eleven

We arrived at the portable Neuralink facility on a mission, and I was not going to leave without answers. The front was clearly marked NEURALINK with LED lights piercing even in daylight. I wouldn't doubt if it was visible from space, no expense was spared on this structure. Thick steel panels riveted with aircraft precision lined the structure in mirroring patterns of geometrical shapes. The roof was a slanted grid of beams supporting thick acrylic skylight sections. I might have taken the time to be impressed if Lucy wasn't pressing on my heart.

Busting through the front entrance and flying up to the receptionist like a Marvel villain, I growled my words, throwing my hands down on the counter, making her flinch.

"Where is the doc?"

"Would you like to schedule a consultation, sir?" she replied, trying to remain professional.

My patience was beyond thin, so I moved my coat to my hip, exposing the arsenal with intent.

"Do I look like I want a consultation?" I said.

Don came up behind me with Chris, their expressions adding to the urgency in my voice.

"Go on in, Ken, I got this," Don said and held his gaze on the young lady. "Everyone clear out," he yelled to the waiting room, waving his shotgun in the air.

Chris held the doors open until the room emptied, then flipped the handle 90 degrees, sliding the locking mechanism into the top jamb and threshold, securing the entrance.

The receptionist must have hit an alert button or intercom notifying the back staff. Connie came through the saloon-hinged doors with a bee in her bonnet.

"What the hell is..." she said, stopping abruptly, staring down the two hollow cylinders of my Remington, knowing the firing pin was a hog's hair twitch away from ending her life.

"Back up slowly. Where's the doctor?" I said, keeping the gun to her nose.

Her eyes did the talking, rolling to one side towards a double set of steel doors, revealing his location.

"How many are in there?" I said, a little quieter this time. Not that it would make a difference.

"Just Dr. Snyder," she said with a quavering voice. My blood boiled at his name. *Snyder*.

"Well, let's go talk to Mr. Snyder," I said, prodding her in the face to lead the way.

Connie pushed through the doors and buckled over a rolling gurney. I shoved her and the gurney to the side as I watched Dr. Snyder bolt out a rear exit. His body flew back unnaturally into the door jamb, crashing to the trailer floor at my feet. John's bulk filled the doorway, blocking the exterior light.

"Good call," he said.

I threw Connie in one of the Neuralink procedure chairs and wondered if it had once contained Lucy. John planted Dr. Snyder in the other.

"Pretty light on security there, don't you think?" I said to Snyder. "Just you and a couple of busty blonds? If I didn't know better, I would think you were a plastic surgeon."

They both just sat there with blank stares. Like children in the principal's office waiting for the paddle.

"I'll tell you what, you're going to start talking," I said and gave a little pause. Looking Snyder straight in the eyes I pulled the trigger. The lead showered his right foot and exposed the crawl space beneath the trailer. He screamed like a school girl and grabbed his shin, pulling it towards his torso. His face was shaking red, pushing instant sweat as I placed the hot barrel to his hairline, forcing him back in the chair.

"You move again and you die," I said with fact in my tone. "Where are they?"

"I... I... I don't know... I... I swear," he spit out with a few extra DNA projectiles.

I paused for a moment and took a much needed breath.

"Let me tell you a little story... When I was a small boy my father bribed me into making my first kill, a beautiful four-point. I just kept thinking of Bambi the whole time. He told me the deer would more than likely not survive the harsh winter even if we let it live. Every year the elements laid waste to thousands of edible game in the very woods that our ancestors foraged for survival. In other words, a mercy killing that could provide enough meat to feed several families. Made sense, but again, I was a child. I did not want to do this, Mr. Snyder. But taking a life was an essential part of becoming a man, I was told... Ten dollars is what it took to get me to pull that trigger. It makes me wonder... Just how much compensation did it take for *you* to pull the trigger on *Lucy*?"

"I didn't pull the..."

Bam. The shotgun ripped toes out of his left shoe, splattering blood up in all directions.

"Oh, that's exactly what you did, you son of a bitch. You turned her over to that fucking sicko."

He was slobbering down his chin, trying to form a verbal response and failing.

"Please," Connie pleaded. "Please, stop. He had to."

"Oh. Now you want to talk," I said. "If his feet are that important to you, how about his little pecker?"

I racked the gun and placed it against his crotch. He wrapped his hands around the barrel and immediately let go, feeling the singe of flesh.

"They're forcing him out," Connie shouted. "Freelance is his only way to stay afloat. Dillon made an offer he couldn't refuse."

Chris came in the room, leading the receptionist by the elbow.

"She's got something to tell you," Chris said and pushed her to her knees next to Connie.

"Somebody had better tell me something and quick," I said, looking from face to face, all of which donned tears of fear to which I had no remorse.

"I arranged transportation last month for Dr. Snyder to meet with Mr. Maxwell," the receptionist said. "It was an address in Sedona."

"Is that right?" I said, looking at Snyder. "I'm impressed, doctor. A man that can endure pain and hold his tongue is rare. Let's just see how much you can bear." His watering eyes locked onto mine. "Don, help me out."

Don pulled the good doctor's head back by the top of his right ear and held a razor sharp combat knife to the lobe. As soon as he began to drag the blade, drawing blood, Snyder started assembling words.

"It's back in the rocks, off the south fork, past the park entrance. I don't have the address. I can take you there," he said with emphasized clarity. "It's an old auto shop."

I motioned Don back with my eyes and he retreated.

"Goodbye, doctor," I said, pulling the trigger on my nine, placing a slug between his eyes without further hesitation. His body went limp and slid to the floor as I looked at the girls. Satisfied with the fear I saw, I holstered the Ruger and concealed the shotgun. "Let's go, I know the shop."

\*\*\*\*\*

Lucy had turned around to go back and look for a cell phone when she heard the ringing. Her hand was on the slider's arm when Joe answered the line. She quickly aborted the thought and ducked into an expansive lounge area with white leather bench seats, low pub tables and a beautiful bar with a solid one-piece white ash top. Mirrored shelves backed the bar that once contained an endless supply of top shelf alcohol, now sparse with an occasional bottle. She slithered out of sight, praying to find some kind of communication device. Even if she found one, based on the condition of the place, she would be skeptical of its functionality, but this was not the time to be a pessimist.

Like a light bulb, she thought of the hovercraft and the possibilities there. But she decided to hide for a bit until the coast was clear. Her mind kept going back to her hands around the knife and the feeling that moved through her arms as the blade plunged through his head. The feeling was of a slow push, then of her dragging the blade back out just to repeat the sensation. She tried to blink it out of her head. *Please stop*, she thought. *This is not me. These are not my thoughts*, she told herself, yet the knife dragged.

"Goddamn it," she yelled, unable to clear the visions. She squeezed the handle of the gun with both hands and pressed the long portion of the barrel to her forehead in a nightmarish prayer.

*****

"The clean-up crew is en route, Dillon's en route, we gotta find that girl," Joe said to his slack-jawed partner, Isaiah. Isaiah shook his head and kissed his crucifix.

"No, sir," he said. "Fuck that, look what she did to them two."

Joe put his hand on his shoulder.

"Believe me. He will do worse if we don't find her. Now put your ear mic in and check the lower decks. I'll check three and four. It's time to man up."

Isaiah took the service elevator to the bottom and left Joe to weather the storm.

"Come here, kitty, kitty," Joe said as he raised a canvas cover of a lifeboat that he doubted could still float. *With the hovercrafts on board, who would use them anyhow*, he thought.

He turned around and peered through the windows of the lounge. It was dark due to the storm and no lights were on. The crew spent most of their time on the bridge when Dillon was away. He was adamant about powering down sections that were not in use. No one could figure why since the yacht was powered through a renewable energy source. He lit up the room with a stinger stream light and the reflection from the glass assaulted his eyes. Quickly he lowered the beam and caught an unusual flicker off the floor just inside the doorway.

"Aha. I've got you, bitch. Water," he said to himself.

He doubled back and went through the state room to access the lounge. With his gun drawn he rounded the corner and quietly squatted next to a French rock statue of a mermaid, polished and preserved to withstand time. A duplicate held up the other end of the massive solid ash top, concealing his mark. He flung his body to the floor and extended his gun and light around the back of the bar, depressing overzealously on the trigger, then backed his finger off before the pin could strike the primer.

Trying to be stealthy, Lucy had slipped through a door at the other end of the bar when she heard Joe. She stood as still as the mermaids, rationing her breath, in a large refrigerator/wine room.

Joe got to his feet, bore down on his molars, hit the lights and surveyed the room like the Terminator while fluorescents blinked to life.

"You think you're tough? Nobody likes a tough girl. Now come on out," he said.

Two rounds exploded the mirror behind him, showering sharp fragments and forcing him to drop and take cover.

"Okay... Maybe I like it a little. Did you count your bullets, young lady?" he asked, pausing for a moment to listen.

"No response was the loud reply," he said to himself, contemplating his next move.

Lucy had fired the rounds through a pass window, giving away her position, and bolted for the door at the opposite end of the room. It led her to a service elevator that only went one way, down. With no other option she took the ride. The box stopped and Lucy slid the gate open to a spacious kitchen which at one time could have been a chef's dream. She imagined fifteen to twenty well-trained servants bustling about like a well-oiled machine. She rocketed through the stainless kitchen and broke into a corridor lined with tiny cabins. Lucy ran like an Olympic contender for the one-hundred-yard dash and ducked into a cabin at the far end of the corridor, putting as much distance between her and her assailant as possible. Shivering and trying to control her hyperventilating, her mind's eye flashed.

# Chapter Twelve

James Boyd Detrick, a retired Master Chief, hit the floor hard and slid across the smooth maple until his momentum was stopped by the unforgiving wall between courts two and three of the Pensacola Racquetball Club. Sweat poured off his head as he laid back in defeat.

"That's it. I'm done," he yelled and rolled to all fours, throwing his racket at the feet of his opponent. "Three losses in a row is my limit."

"Come on, old man, don't be sore. You whooped me like a redheaded stepchild last week, remember?" his regular Wednesday night opponent said.

"You popping stimulants, Miller? Let me see your eyes."

"One hundred percent drug free, senior," Miller said and reached out to help him to his feet.

"I'll beat you straight up, you son of a bitch. Now let's go, twenty minutes until happy hour," James said, swatting Miller's hand away like a mother would to a four-year-old for stealing cookies from the jar. He dropped down to his chest, pumped out a few military style pushups and began a series of post 'got my ass handed to me but it won't happen again' stretches.

"Are Woody and the Proctor going to be there?" James asked as he retrieved his racket and wiped his face of protruding salt.

"The Admiral will be there, yes. And don't call him that, dude."

"He's retired and the shoe fits."

"It makes me uncomfortable," Miller confessed. "Everything about the man intimidates me."

"For Christ's sake, kid. You went through BUDS. Besides, he likes ya. Don't worry, we'll get him liquored up and make him do something stupid so you have some dirt on him. How's that sound?"

Miller was a good-looking kid who reminded James of his son Ken. Tall and fit with a controlled aggressive attitude which you would be hard pressed not to respect. He was an asset to any mission and would die for his beloved country at the drop of a hat. The only thing grounding Miller with the geriatrics was a mild seizure disorder, brought about by an old friend named shrapnel.

Miller could never tell when Detrick was serious or not. But he would not put it past him to blackmail a friend for grins. Hell, he probably had dirt on every one of them.

"That doesn't sound good, man," Miller said.

"That's how we do things here, son. You know what they say, when in Rome."

"I hate that phrase. It's like the one my momma always used." He changed his voice to a high pitched nag you couldn't help but laugh at. "If your friends were jumping off a cliff, would you?"

"Well, I ain't your momma, young whipper-snapper, and you a long way from Montana. Plus, I know the answer to that question."

"Hell, yeah," they said in unison.

"Now serve, so I can gain back some dignity here. Then we can go face your fears and have a beer with the Proctor. Besides, he owes me a Cuban."

*****

Chris had insisted on joining our venture out of Vegas, which surprised me. She said she was in it for the long haul and somehow felt a responsibility for Lucy. I wasn't going to argue, especially after she offered the use of a company hovercraft. She was an excellent pilot, maneuvering us out of the city skyscrapers, opposing crafts and blockades for the aerial shows.

We set down safely in Barstow to retrieve our gliders and were back in the sky within minutes. Looking off to the north I could see earth's massive scar, a beautiful and intense sight, displaying the power of Mother Nature. I couldn't help but think of the many souls that perished in the depths of the red rock canyon bordering Utah, Arizona and Nevada. I believed with all my heart that Lucy was not one of them, but at this point there was no way of knowing.

"Don? You got your ears on?" I asked as I dropped altitude, leading the pack.

"Still here, what's on your mind?" he replied.

"How much time do you think we have?"

"You mean, how long do I think Lucy can hold out? There's no telling, Ken. Try not to think of that one, okay?"

"Well, I know we can't be that far behind 'em."

"We don't know that she's at this location. Keep that in mind. Guns blaze and she's not, they could alert this Dillon guy that we're onto them."

"Good point. Okay, let's touch down at the airport and get our bearings. There are some old abandoned hangars towards the back, right off the river. It's not far from the shop and will provide some cover for now."

"Your lead, big dog."

*****

"Intelligence is the key to warfare, always has been. That and the element of surprise. But you can bet your ass, if you have intel on them, they have intel on you. And that's the crazy part," Admiral Sheldon stated. He looked over to Miller and compacted his eyes. "You a mole, Miller?"

"No, sir. No mole, sir," Miller said.

"It's always the good ones, the ones with charisma. Snowball. That's what I call it. Snowball."

The Admiral cocked a bushy eyebrow at Miller, making him feel even more uncomfortable, and held the look as if waiting for a response.

"Well, I'll take that as a compliment, sir," Miller finally said.

"Did you see this thing about a merger?" James said, pointing to the flat screen over the bar.

The tension broke as they all turned to look at the news clip.

"Oh yeah, that guy Portman is a real-life Tony Stark, he's got more money than God," Woody said and took a swig of draft.

"I watched the demo on the energy launcher earlier. Amazing. Someone was using their noggin. The military contract alone will be off the charts," Sheldon said, sidetracked from his interrogation of young Miller.

"Don't you find it odd? Why merge companies? It makes no sense, even if it's just one product line. I've never even heard of

Maxwell Industries, now Portman publicly announces a merger," James said.

Admiral Sheldon answered, "I'll tell you what. Everything this guy has ever done was for a reason. You don't get where he is in life by letting guys push you around. Politics, my friend. If all Portman wanted was that launcher, he would have tactically taken it. This is political."

They looked back to the TV as the camera zoomed in on the EL40, and listened to the narrator describe the nomenclature of the weapon with a brief understanding of how it works.

James got up and popped the Proctor in the shoulder with an opened hand and grabbed his Cognac with his other.

"Come on, smoke time," he said and gestured for them to follow.

They took their drinks to the cigar room in the back off the patio. With a plush interior and a panoramic view of the Gulf of Mexico, it provided a genuine 'life is good' feel. They sank into soft leather chairs with audible pleasure while the hostess greeted them by name, offering an array of hand-rolled cigars. With a mobile humidor in hand she made her rounds, clipped their picks and left a tray of small wooden matches to light at leisure. A fire warmed the room from the corner while a cold rain brushed the windows with light to heavy bursts, pulling the storm from the sea.

"It's only going to get worse," the Proctor said as he bit down with exposed teeth on his cigar.

"The weatherman sure got it wrong this time," Woody said. "Straight from blue skies to hurricane warnings."

James lit his cigar and looked out at the rain soaking the patio furniture. A wake of water beyond an aircraft carrier, almost unrecognizable from the chop, drew his attention, causing his mind to drift.

"Good stuff, huh?" the Proctor said, blowing a smoke ring with perfection. "Earth to James."

"Just glad to be grounded on a night like this," James said, snapping from his trance. He raised his glass for a toast. "To good cigars and good friends, old and new, salute."

"All right, enough of the terms of endearment shit," the Admiral said, looking over his shoulder to make sure they were alone in their conversation. "You know things are going to get real ugly if this technology gets in the wrong hands; Southwest China, Russia, Eastern regimes, you name it."

"Sheldon, your hair is already grey. You've done your time. What are we going to do, call the Council on Foreign Relations and start World War III? We've already stressed enough for two lifetimes, my friend. Now smoke your cigar in the serenity you've earned," James said.

"We've got two names, Portman and Maxwell. It's a place to start."

"For the love of country, old man, stop," James said, but the two names had already entered his mind while staring at the wake of his country's muscle.

*****

"Why did you do it, Dillon?" the teacher asked with pursed lips of frustration.

A nine-year-old boy sat in the principal's office once more, staring at his own feet. An emergency panel of teachers and crisis counselors questioned him like an FBI interrogation. He was trapped, yet unusually calm.

"Ty made me do it," Dillon said, without removing his eyes from his left shoelace.

"Your brother made you do it? Is that the story you're going with?" the teacher asked.

"I can make him do things too," Dillon said, grinning at the thought.

"You can't touch girls like that, Dillon," one of the counselors added. "It's inappropriate and we have a zero tolerance policy in this district that we take very seriously."

"Why is it that you only act up when you have a female teacher? Miss Ainsworth has subbed your class three times this year and each time you have ended up here," the principal said.

"You are a sick little boy," Miss Ainsworth said. "And when your parents get here you are going to describe to them exactly what you did to that little…"

Dillon sprung from his seat, wrapped his fingers around the stapler on the desk and before anyone could restrain him, smashed it into Miss Ainsworth's face, caving in her rather large nose. Blood splattered about the room as she pulled her head back and screamed in carnal agony.

Lucy saw the image of young Dillon's fingers around the stapler, blood dripping from the knuckles. It was as if the fingers were her own. Miss Ainsworth's face flashed in her mind, flinging back, spraying blood… Then her fingers dripped again. She felt a pulling sensation as if she liked the fresh blood and craved to lick it from her fingers for satisfaction. She shook her head in confused disgust.

"Ty made me do it," she heard in young Dillon's voice. "I can make him do things too."

"Come out, come out, wherever you are," interrupted the chaos, but the voice was different this time, evil, like Cape Fear.

Joe was going room by room tossing beds, kicking doors, ripping shower curtains. She could hear him getting closer, taunting with aggressive movement.

"You can run but you can't hide. Or might I say, you can hide but you can't run. Come on out, Lucy, make it easy on yourself," he said.

Lucy spotted an access panel in the bathroom. It looked to be some kind of plumbing chase. She pried it open and stuck her head in to explore. Cracks of light penetrated the shaft from above and below with pipes and insulated wire running down the center. *I think I can make it*, she thought. Her mind was a little clearer now, free from the monster within. The flashes came and went with no regularity so she had to move now while she could rationalize her actions. She thought small, slipped her body around the piping and pulled the thin panel into place. It was so tight that her chest was separated, pipe snug to her sternum, her chin was pinned to one side and her back was against the rusted chase wall. Rivets tore at her shirt as she inched her way down. *I should have just shot his ass*, she thought as claustrophobia joined her.

"Isaiah, check the quarters below the kitchen," Joe said into his mic.

"That's what I'm doing, no luck," he responded.

"Go back through just in case," Joe said, checking the last room and coming up short.

"Yes, sir," he said, *whatever you say*.

Lucy's feet touched bottom and her legs were forced to bend, punching her feet through a flimsy rusted panel. She forced the rest of her legs to follow, cutting her thighs until her hands pushed the remainder of the panel free. She gripped the top jamb of the access door and took a moment to get her breathing calmed and heart rate down. Her pulse continued to thunder in her temples. She had never been this scared in her life.

Tired and disoriented, she slithered out from the bowels of The Claiborne and lay on a gritty floor of filth smelling of musk and mold. Realizing that she was in a mop closet in the colon of the beast, she quickly got to her feet, shivering from head to toe in disgust. The walls were iron, moist and rough with rust. The blackness of the room made her panic and push at the heavy door vigorously. Breaking the rust bond, a crack of light greeted Lucy, marginally subsiding her panic. Gaining her composure she mustered the courage and peeked out through the thin sliver of luminance. Few lights dimly cast over another corroded iron hallway resembling what Lucy thought could be a green mile to purgatory. She dropped the mag from the Glock into her hand, and using the faint light, counted the rounds, reinserted and chambered. The movements came as second nature. She blinked it off.

"Now or never," she told herself, popped the door open with a shoulder shove and moved through the hall with the gun raised at the ready.

Lucy slowed down and took in her surroundings. Doors had been replaced with welded rod, creating cells -- small, damp cells.

Squinting her eyes to adjust to the light, she peered in each one as she moved along the wall at a snail's pace.

"What are you doing?" a voice said from the cell behind her.

Lucy turned and saw a young girl on the floor with her face pressed to the bars that held her captive.

"Oh my God," Lucy said, "Are you all right?"

The girl closed her eyes for a moment, paused and then opened them slowly about halfway, as if drug induced.

"I've been better," she rasped.

It was obvious to Lucy that she had been drugged with a type of suppressant and her heart strings pulled.

"What's your name, sweetie? Are you alone?"
"Sh-Sheila," she whispered. "There are three... Three of us right now."

Two more young faces came into the light; three girls, three separate cells.

"How long have you been down here? We have to get you out," Lucy said and started looking around for something to pick the locks with.

"No," Sheila said in a panic. "No, don't. He'll kill us."

There was no doubt in Lucy's mind that these girls would not live long in this environment. Judging by their tattered bodies and sunken faces, in no more than a week or two, they would be done.

"You can't stay in here, Sheila. You will die for sure."

"If he likes you then he keeps you alive, you just have to please," she muttered.

"Listen, if he's taking more girls then eventually he will have no need for you. The drugs are clouding your thoughts."

"He likes to smell you. He likes the way I smell," one of the other girls said in a soft, broken trance.

Lucy looked from face to face. Dirty tear-marked cheeks, long-dried from sedation and lack of will to wipe them away. Wrists and ankles bloody and bruised, sore to the touch if not for the drugs. Breasts and throats discolored from over attention by their captors. More than one monster had had his hands on these girls. Lucy's heart broke, fear for their survival as well as her own surfaced in her throat like devil's bile. She closed her eyes in frustration and swallowed what little saliva she had generated to combat the up-turn.

"I'm Rebecca and this is Carmen," Rebecca's monotone voice creaked. "She doesn't speak. We don't know for sure, but we think he might have cut her tongue out."

Carmen definitely looked in worse shape than the others.

"What are they giving you?" Lucy asked Rebecca, looking into blacked eyes.

She showed Lucy her arms with shame in her movement, exposing tracks of bruised veins and fresh scabbed portholes. The points of entry were pulsating as if reaching for the needle. Begging for it as she practically hyperextended the arm pushing it through the bars.

"Heroin… It's part of his game. He'll get you to beg for it."

"This is not a game, far from it." Lucy looked around. "I'm going to get you out of here. I'm going to get help," she said and started to move on.

"Wait," Sheila said. "What's your name?"

The door at the end of the run opened with an audible creak of a neglected hinge. Isaiah approached the occupied cells and looked in at Sheila. She had backed away from the bars and pulled her knees to her chest.

"Who are you talking to, She-ra?" he said.

She kept her head down, staying silent as he stepped to the next cell.

"Is she still here?" he asked.

Rebecca gave him the same response so he moved on.

"I think she is," he said and knelt down to Carmen who was still at the door. He showed her a syringe and ran the back of his finger down her cheek.

"Carmen? Which way, Carmen?" he said softly to his favorite.

Her eyes rolled to the right and slowly back to the syringe.

Isaiah looked in that direction, got to his feet and continued down the cell fronts. Carmen dropped her head, secretly hoping for the return of the black heat.

Gun raised, Isaiah moved slowly, checking each cell, every nook, and every shadow. The end of the run opened to a small area with a couple of desks, some foot lockers, a TV and a refrigerator lined with nude photos of the most promising. He stopped short of the office and held his position knowing she was there, while the bodies of Tony and Enriquez came to his mind's eye, making this one personal.

Lucy was shaking under a large scarred oak desk as Isaiah approached. She shuffled her hand position on the gun grip to wipe the sweat from her palms. Squinting her eyes she drew in a deep breath and tried to calm her pounding heart. Every sound was amplified including the scuff and drag of Isaiah's boots on the littered diamond plate. Lucy was boxed in. The time to fight or flight was now and flight was no longer an option. She braced her feet flat on the floor and leaned her body weight forward when she heard his slithering voice replace the drag.

"Are you a religious woman, Lucy?" he asked with a mischievous tone.

She did not answer him. Only the drum of the ship stressing from the storm could be heard.

"There is a passage I would like to share with you...
'Submit yourself to the Lord. Resist the Devil and he will flee from you.' Now the question you have to ask yourself, Lucy, is who is the Lord? And who is the Devil?"

He shifted around the corner into the room as Lucy popped up from behind the desk with her gun raised. Isaiah slammed his boot into the desk, driving it back into Lucy's ribs, crushing her against the refrigerator door. Her gun hand flew back as a bullet grazed Isaiah's shoulder. He came across the desk, grabbed her right arm and pinned it to the redhead on the fridge, forcing the gun to come free and topple to the floor. His fist came down hard on the bridge of Lucy's nose and turned the lights out with a crack, flopping her unconscious head back denting the freezer, then collapsing her body forward to the desktop in an unnatural position. Isaiah threw the desk across the room with one hand and pushed her body to the floor with the other. He forced her wrists into restraints as quickly as possible, fearing the resurrection of the devil within. Enriquez's lifeless eyes flashed as he rolled her to her back. He took in his moment of victory... looked her body over from head to toe... then keyed his mic.

"I got her, Joe. I'll bring her up. Where do you want her?"

"Take her to the state room until we get this mess cleaned up. I'll meet you there," Joe said with obvious relief in his voice.

# Chapter Thirteen

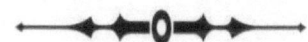

Chris was following close behind Don and John. I wasn't sure exactly how I felt about her tagging along. Was she going to hinder or help our situation? All I knew at this point was that without her we wouldn't be this close. Besides, without knowing what lay ahead, every helping hand should be welcome.

We rounded a rock formation that reminded me of a wine bottle filled with layers of colored sand jutting into the sky and reaching out for the heavens. It always felt like I was on another planet flying into this area. The terrain of the high desert was like no other on earth, unforgiving yet breathtaking.

The crevices in the rock gave shelter to many less fortunate people. Typically they were outcasts of a not-so-higher society, forced into thievery for survival as begging did not work in these times. Earth's bandits, pirates of the rock, clad in burlap from the red gravel yards, the villains of childhood story books disrupting the dreams of many a young. They were stealthy and dangerous people with eyes constantly locked on the sky. I don't know how they communicated so fast with such a primal lifestyle but it didn't take them long to descend on the rusted hangar when we touched down in their domain.

"Ken, you're not planning on leaving our crafts here, are you?" Chris said as we cut power and put foot to ground.

"We're just going to do some surveillance work, missy. We can't just fly in like a fighter battalion and risk being spotted. And don't worry about these people, they saw us coming fifty miles back."

"Damn straight we saw you," a voice boomed from the thick.

Resembling a pack of wolves with thirsty eyes fixed on their prey, they appeared like ghosts out of the dusty air, surrounding us with numbers.

"Easy now," I said, drawing my hands above my shoulders. "We're going to need to use this hangar for a bit and then we'll be out of your way."

"Is that a fact, pretty boy," one said and moved his body to invade my space, which he clearly thought was his to invade.

John's posture changed in an instant to match this man's fury. I quickly placed my right hand on John's chest to keep him at bay and took a deep breath. I could feel the cold steel of an assault rifle brush the coarse stubble on my chin. The man was shorter than I, with a fragile physique under tattered garments that needed to be burned rather than laundered. His determination and his fearlessness were his strengths. And his eyes spoke a thousand words. Bloodshot and wind-blown, they glared at me from under a stern brow, daring me to make a move. I had clearly underestimated these folks and needed to rethink my strategy. 'Money talks and bullshit walks' came to mind. My father used to add 'Said the rock people' to the end of that phrase. I believe he was referring to the people before me.

"We didn't come here to shed blood," I said, keeping eye contact. "But you're picking a fight that no one wins."

I could feel his finger tense on the trigger. He pulled my jacket open with his free hand, exposing my steel.

"I'm not as stupid as I look… that's exactly what you came to do."

"These bullets are not meant for you, my friend. Now lower that weapon and we can talk compensation."

His eyes rolled to the left past John and landed on Chris for a moment while wheels turned in his simple mind.

"We might be able to make a deal," he said, lowering the rifle muzzle to the ground. He looked at Don and John. "What are you, the beanstalk twins?"

"Very funny. I take shits bigger than you," John said.

The fiery man moved to raise the weapon and I quickly intervened.

"Whoa," I said, gesturing to take a walk. "Let's talk business, shall we?"

Rock man took my suggestion and moved towards an opening in the back of the hangar. I fell into step beside him and glanced back at John with a quizzical 'what the fuck' look. We walked outside the structure before the conversation continued.

"Name's Wally," he said. "You attached to the girl?" His bluntness did not surprise me.

"Wally? It ain't going to happen... I do have some money I'm willing to part with for your services though. You can call me Ken."

He looked up at me and smiled a rotten, semi-toothy grin.

"Well, it's my lucky day then," he said. "Does this have anything to do with the brick place over yonder?"

"As a matter of fact, what do you know there, Wally?"

"Call me Walt. Any foe of that fuck Dillon is a friend of mine."

"Okay, Walt. Has there been some movement there today?"

He paused and held his hand out. It was rough and filthy like an auto mechanic after a hard day's work. I placed a hundred dollar bill in his palm and he shoved it in his pocket as he spoke.

"Two of them crafts like you got came in 'bout an hour ago. Then just before you arrived two left. Bigger ones and they left in a hurry. I mean, gone in the blink of an eye."

"Did you see a girl, by chance?"

He held his hand out once more and looked up at the sky. I placed another bill down and snapped him from his trance.

"Nope, no girl. I would have noticed one of them. But I can't very well see in dem crafts now, can I?"

"I need you to be helpful now, Walt."

"I answered your question."

"What kind of security do they have?"

"Security? What the hell do they need that for? They got so many guns and shit in there, it's like an armory. And there are always guys in there, they never leave the place alone."

"Except today, because you saw a bunch leave?"

"I saw two craf…" He stopped himself, pursed his dried lips and held his hand out again.

I slapped three more bills down, one after another.

"Spill," I said with irritation in my voice.

"I said I saw two crafts. I'm sure they were haulin' crews but I guarantee you they didn't leave that place empty. No siree, Bob."

"How about video surveillance?"

"They got cameras. I don't know if they watch 'em. You would have to be stupid to try and break in there anyway; all those boys know how to shoot. They come out here and shoot up the rocks all the time for practice."

"I need to get a look at this place, Walt. What's the best vantage point? Somewhere I can take a glider and not be seen."

We walked to the top of a low plateau of crumbly soil and he pointed to the southeast through a gap in the slate rock horizon. "Right there," he said. "Hug the ground, though. You can touch down by that L-shaped rock and it's just a short hike around the bend."

"Good. I need to leave that hovercraft here for now. Will a thousand do?"

"A thousand bucks with no bloodshed. You've got yourself a deal."

"Half now and the other half when we leave your back yard with that craft in the same condition it's in now. Capeesh?"

"Capeesh."

We left Portman's company craft in the hands of Walt and his creepy crew and took the two gliders to the lookout point. Chris rode with me, making me think of Lucy, not that she wasn't already on my mind.

"I think Walt fancies you," I said to Chris, teasing.

"Don't start, Ken, it's not funny. They give me the heebies."

We snaked on our bellies around the bend that Walt had pointed out and came to a halt before a breathtaking view of the river cutting through the rock formations below. I brought the Oberwerk high powered binoculars to my eyes and spent a minute focusing in on Dillon's garage. I needed as clear a picture as possible. Don and John had already locked in on our target. Don with Skyhawk Ultra binoculars and John through his optic scope as usual, finger always on the trigger, helping him balance. Chris nudged my arm for a look and I shushed her. The sun was setting but not fast enough. We were going to have to hit this place after dark and time was nothing short of agonizing. I couldn't bear the thought of what Lucy was going through. If she was still alive, that is. Several minutes passed before anyone spoke.

"There's got to be dogs down there," Don said. "Did Walt say anything about dogs?"

"Nope, he said there was no security, just a bunch of cowboys that know how to use their high powered six shooters," I said.

"They've got cameras on the roof, Ken. Looks like all the points of entry are covered. If someone is half paying attention they're going to see us coming," John said.

A small pedestrian door opened off the side of the building and a large hairy man stepped out lighting a cigarette. He blew a cloud and looked up in our direction.

"He doesn't see us, we're in a shadow," Don said.

A second man stepped out, every bit as ugly, and the two exchanged words. He was throwing his hands up and looking towards the sky, obviously pissed about something. He clearly didn't approve of the man being outside. The hairy smoker surrendered, flicked his cigarette at a heap of rusted metal and followed his partner back in the building, pausing one last time to look up at the heavens before slamming the door behind him.

"Well, I think that answers the question," I said. "They're going to see us coming."

"Let's go back to the hangar and work this out. You know we're going to have to wait for the sandman anyway," Don said.

*****

Dillon and Jax were approaching The Claiborne shortly after the crews from Sedona. Dillon was heated and distraught over Tony and Enriquez, yet with slightly subsided anger at word of Lucy's containment.

"I'll take care of the disposal, Dillon," Jax said. "Go ahead and check on Lucy. They have her in the state room for now."

"I want to see the bodies myself, Jax. Go sit on Lucy for me. Make sure she doesn't slip again. I'll meet you there."

Rain was coming down in sheets like drums of water were being dumped from the sky by angry gods. The ship was descending hard off the top of the ocean swells just to rise again for the next. Landings were difficult but manageable with the use of the laser-guided assist. Tommy and Patrick were securing the hovercraft and taking a beating from the storm, but they were fast and efficient, navigating the ship like they were on solid ground. As soon as Dillon's glider made contact Tommy went to work adjusting the vises and aligning the cleats while Patrick pulled the cover. Dillon and Jax hit the deck running, in part to get out of the harsh elements, but mainly to handle business. Dillon would not rest until order was restored.

He entered the suite, pulled a bottle of Jack from the bar, popped the top and took a long draw as he surveyed the damage. His crew was standing aside, giving him the space he needed. Dillon was not a heartfelt man, but Enriquez was one of his most trusted men and one of the few he considered to be a friend, and they all knew it.

Dillon turned from the bar and walked towards Tony with bottle in hand. Standing over his corpse he turned the bottle upside down, splashing his open chest and giving him one last bit of the sailor's nectar. He turned and pushed open the door to the bath, exposing Enriquez. Stepping through the blood Dillon straddled his body and look down into his friend's lifeless eyes. A moment of silence was in order.

The silence inspired thought, thoughts of Lucy. He drew their minds together. *Welcome back, Lucy. Two can play at this game.*

He was never quite sure if his thoughts came through as feelings or words, but one thing was certain, his meaning would be clear. That was the beauty of the connection. And it was a two-way street, so he could enjoy every bit of the fear which he instilled.

Dillon set the bottle of Jack on the counter and leaned in to better his position. He placed his boot on Enriquez's forehead, bore down and pulled the knife free with both hands. He thought he heard a gasp but it was just the sound of steel sliding through flesh and coagulating fluid. Wasting no more time, he cleaned the blood from the blade and handle with a towel, said his goodbyes, wiped the blood from his boot soles and calmly left the carnage to tend to his Lucy.

"Okay boys, spotless, and let me know when it's ready," Dillon said and handed off the bottle as he exited the suite.

Lucy had been stripped down, cleaned the best they could and dressed in a cotton nighty. It was tight to her body, extra thin around her nipples and bunched up on her hips. A yellow happy face with a bullet hole between the eyes bled down her left breast. She lay back on a low plush armless chair with her ankles restrained by iron brackets mounted to the floor on either side. Her hands were clamped together on a slide rod behind her head, running from floor to ceiling. Jax stood shaking his head as Joe tried to explain the situation.

"Don't waste your breath, Joe," Jax said, as Dillon stepped through the door, closed it firmly behind him and looked at Lucy. She stared back with watery eyes of hate behind blackened flesh and a busted and swollen nose.

Joe blurted out his plea, "Dillon, she went crazy, you saw what she…" but was stopped short by the barrel of a 357. Dillon had drawn the weapon and held it inches from Joe's face. The pause was just long enough for Joe to swallow his saliva audibly before the bullet popped through his skull and blew the back of his scalp across the room. His body jerked back slightly and fell to the floor like a sandbag.

Nobody said a word as the sound continued ringing eardrums. Dillon breathed in through his nose and exhaled through puffed cheeks with his eyes closed. This act of spontaneous violence only pacified a small fraction of his frustration. He opened them slowly and glared back at Lucy as he spoke.

"Jax, get him out of here and take his scalp with him. Oh, and Isaiah?"

"Yes, sir," Isaiah managed to squeak out.

"Get me Sheila."

"Yes, sir."

"Isaiah? Before you go, give me one of those ancient proverbs you're always rambling about."

"A warrior is not born," Isaiah said with his head down, mourning the loss of a friend. He raised his eyes to meet Dillon's as he finished the phrase, "He is made from God's tears… and the Devil's fury."

Dillon nodded his approval. "You are a fine warrior, Isaiah. Now fetch me Sheila."

Isaiah took the same wheelchair he had brought Lucy up with and returned to the bowels of The Claiborne feeling like more of a coward than a warrior.

Jax rolled Joe's body up in what once had been a beautiful Persian rug. Worn with age and soaked with blood, the Persian masterpiece would now face the same fate as Joe. Jax dragged the pig-in-a-blanket over the threshold and called Tommy to assist as he closed the door behind him.

"Alone at last," Dillon said. "Have you enjoyed your time on my boat so far, Lucy?"

Her body was tense and her chest was rising and falling with each breath. She glared at Dillon and chose not to gratify him with a response.

"You really need to relax, hon. You've been making my heart race since Vegas."

Dillon sat down at a low table next to Lucy and pulled himself up close so their legs touched. Lucy knew better than to flinch. He pulled a black leather hype kit from his BDU pants side pocket and gently splayed it across the table. His movements were in a delayed timeframe, intensifying the dread she felt within. He spoke slowly, preparing the needle with black tar while basking in every palpable vibe Lucy involuntarily sent to his core.

"Do you enjoy my thoughts, Lucy? I have shared some of my fondest memories… You are a tough young lady, Lucy, I'll give you that… Well, hopefully our link will get even stronger with time. We'll start out slow and easy for you but you're gonna need to participate a little, okay?" He flicked the syringe and depressed the air out. With one eye closed he aligned the needle point with the gaze that he and Lucy held. "That's it… Let me feel your fear, tell me, baby."

"No… no…," she said, shaking her head. "Please don't." Tears streamed down her face with a pleading thought… *Ken*.

"It won't do you any good to think of him," Dillon said. "He will never find you. I know our coordinates and still have trouble finding it."

He patted the inside of her bare thigh with his rough hand, pushed his fingers towards her privates and whispered, "Let's put your mind at ease, honey, but me first, you'll have to wait your turn."

He dropped the syringe on the seat and dragged his fingers up, lingering to feel her warmth and moisture… then brought the pads of his index and middle finger to his nostrils to savor her scent.

Lucy shook with a loathing she never imagined.

Wasting no more time Dillon got down to business grabbing the rubber cord from the kit, wrapping his left bicep and pulling tight with his teeth to make the slip knot.

"Watch Lucy, so you know how to do it," he said out of the corner of his mouth.

He pumped his fist to draw the vein, picked up the syringe and brought it to his arm. As he steadied his right hand on his left forearm he injected the needle into its familiar track with a slow, even push. Dillon's body drank the warm molasses as if it was dying of thirst. He released the strap and laid his head back to look at the ceiling, but his eyes just rolled in their lids.

"Do you feel that, Lucy?" he said, holding his position, still fading to bliss.

Isaiah knocked on the door and announced himself.

"Boss? Isaiah."

Dillon did not answer.

"Dillon?" he said a little louder. "I've got Sheila."

"Come in," Lucy blurted out, trying to fight back her tears. She was feeling her body and mind calm but wasn't sure if it was due to the heroin Dillon injected or the fact that his attention had been temporarily averted.

Isaiah pushed Sheila into the room. Her body was slumped over in the wheelchair as if she were sleeping, but Lucy knew better. She had been fed the black poison they all liked so much, probably begged for it. He looked at Dillon for a second. And with his condition being of no surprise to him, carried on with normality, moving Sheila's limp figure to an identical restraint chair facing Lucy. He placed her in the chair, spreading her legs out, manipulating her body like a sleeping child. He fastened her ankles, pulled her arms up above her head and clamped her wrists into the slide. Pulling her nightgown up over her breasts, he exposed her frail, abused body. Isaiah pinched Sheila's left nipple hard, leaving white finger impressions as he looked her body over in a final farewell, moment shared. With a bit of disappointment on his face he glanced at Lucy, as if to say 'You fucked this up' and exited the room with his head down.

"Sheila?" Lucy called. "Sheila?" a little louder.

She did not respond but her hips shifted to one side then back, thus telling Lucy she was alive.

"I'm sorry, Sheila," Lucy said under her breath.

Dillon suddenly faced forward, drawing in a deep breath, held it for a moment and exhaled, opening his eyes wide to Lucy.

He rose slowly to his feet with the help of his arms and walked five or six feet to Sheila's side and turned around.

"So I understand that you two have met," he said and knelt down beside her. "She was a beautiful, young, healthy thing, Lucy. You should have seen her. It's a shame it has come to this."

Dillon tapped out a small vial of white powder onto Sheila's leg. He unsheathed the knife he had recently pulled from his dead friend's head and proceeded to line the cocaine with the sharpness of the blade.

"Does this look familiar?" he said with menace.

Lucy trembled from head to toe at the realization. This was no longer a mind game between her and this monster. He was real, in the flesh, dangerous beyond all means and steel flashed before her eyes.

Dillon bent over, put a finger to a nostril and snorted the line of stimulant from her hip to her knee, looking up at Lucy with a clenched jaw and black eyes the size of quarters.

"Mmmm… Nothing better," he said and shook his head vigorously.

Flashes of Sheila's naked body came into Lucy's mind. One clean, beautiful, flawless, without bruises or track marks; the next splattered with bright blood, fresh from the vein, covering her from knotted hair to chipped toenails.

"Don't," Lucy pleaded. "Don't do it, Dillon. Leave her alone, please. Leave her alone."

Dillon pulled down hard on the cable pulley system, drawing Sheila's hands up on the slide rod, stretching her thin body and forcing a cry from her weak lungs. He placed the tip of the knife under her chin and sniffed the flesh of her neck and ear.

"She still smells of lavender. Such a refreshing scent," he said.

"I'll do whatever you want, Dillon. Don't," Lucy pleaded.

His hands eased up on the cable, causing Sheila's body to lower to the tip of the knife, penetrating the flesh under her chin, drawing blood.

"Does this look familiar, Lucy?" he said. "You better start answering me."

"Yes," she said. Sheila's blood-covered image flashed again. "Now stop, Dillon."

He let go of the cable and drove the blade through her brain. Blood ran down his forearm, covering her as he looked back over his shoulder at Lucy with a crinkled nose and exposed teeth. Blood oozed from her eyes and nose, adding to the horror of death. Her lifeless body hung from the quillon of the knife suspended by Dillon's muscular blood-covered arm as he stared.

"Feel the life drain, Lucy," he said. "Like you did with Enriquez."

## Chapter Fourteen

The night was cool with very little natural light penetrating the dark sky. The welcome smell of rain was in the air but had yet to show its face. *Anything to knock the dust down,* Ken thought. Don and John were trying to get some rest so they would be alert when we hit Dillon's Sedona garage. Chris and I, on the other hand, had spinning minds that would not allow slumber. So we sat by the fire with Walt and a couple of other shady looking characters, going over our plan of attack. Three AM go time was approaching and I was struggling with the wait.

"They've got to be out by now," I said. "I'll bet nobody's even watching the monitors."

"Yeah, but you know as soon as you blow the roof it won't matter. The hornets' nest will be stirred," Chris said.

"That's the idea. You sure you want to go in?"

"Ken, if Lucy is in there… well, you know. I need to be there."

"It sounds like it's a skeleton crew. I don't think she's there, Chris. But I need info so we can't just go shooting everybody. That puts us at more of a risk."

"I understand the risk, Ken, I'm going."

"Enough said. As a matter of fact, it's three o'clock somewhere. Wake the boys, let's get this over with."

Chris jumped to her feet, dusted off her pant legs and went to the hangar to get strapped.

"Well, Walt. This is it," I said as we both got to our feet.

"Don't you worry 'bout a thing Mr. Ken, we've got your back on the ground level. My guys are already in position and no one will touch your hovercraft. My word," Walt said.

"I appreciate this. Remember to keep your distance though. I don't want any of your men in harm's way."

"Snipers only, I don't want any of those assholes coming this way anyhow. I'm just protectin' my own."

"Good deal, Walt," I said and shook his hand.

When I got to the hangar my crew was ready to go. Loaded down, they looked like a SEAL team ready for the most important mission of their lives. And it gave me faith.

"These guys won't know what hit 'em," I said, grabbing Chris by the vest.

I gave her a few tugs and a pull, checked the contents of her vest and mouthed the words, thank you.

"Don't thank me yet," she said.

I strapped on my gear and gave Don and John a fist pump. "Let's ride," I said.

Don and John set their glider down at the same vantage point we were at earlier and hiked to the mark on foot. Chris piloted my Ducati and we made a pass over the building, killing the lights. At least all that we could. The magnetic field controlling the craft created a dull blue hue of its own. Only when we killed the power so I could eject did it dissipate. I pulled my chute and glided towards the garage roof in silence. It was a quick drop of only about two thousand feet, taking less than a minute to hit the corner of my target with a smooth landing. I pulled the chute in and did a quick tie to conceal it. The roof mounted cameras were pointed at the sky so as long as they didn't detect the drop I was in the clear. *Oh my God, what idiots.*

I moved quietly but worked fast setting up the retractable roof panel with C-4 explosives. The result consisted of eight small bricks of plastic, one at each structure point, wired to a common receiver for remote detonation. Moving to the stairwell door I looked back briefly to admire my work. After checking the lock on the ped-door and confirming my assumption, I rolled a golf ball, packed the dead bolt and inserted the last wire for quick entry. Ahead of schedule, I rested my back against the used concrete brick that created the pony wall perimeter of the building. Looking at the two-ton iron roof hatch, squinting my eyes to clear my vision, I following each wire connecting the dots in my mind, *looks good Ken*, and keyed my mic.

"Roof is ready, over."

"Ten-four, rubber ducky, about two mics out, any movement?" Don returned.

"Negative, all's a go."

I took a breather for another minute then anchored my rappel gear. With phase one complete I threw my body over the edge and pushed off. Skimming down the east side of the building I stopped only once to redirect one of the east mount security cameras to the sky. Not that it would make any difference. All would be awake soon enough. My feet hit dirt and I pushed C-4 into the hinges and strike of the east steel pedestrian door, then rounded the corner to get a visual on Don and John.

John quickly gave the thumbs up gesture after making eye contact, indicating that their targets were wired as well. The three of us took cover in our preset locations amongst the scrap yard and braced for detonation.

"On five," I said into the mic but held off from the countdown. The door I had just wired cracked open to a forty-five, breaking the connection to the strike, and a man stumbled out obviously intoxicated.

"What you waitin' on?" John impatiently blurted.

"Hold the traffic," I said. "We've got movement."

Don and John could not see him from their positions.
The man moved just behind the door, leaving it open, and proceeded to urinate where he stood. It was clear our cover was still good so I whispered the count.

"Five, four, three, two, one." *Blast off.*

The explosions went at the same time, blowing out doors and windows and caving the roof in with four thousand pounds of iron. God speed anyone within the trajectory of the roof hatch. I knew Lucy wasn't in there and could care less how many I had to kill to find out where she was. I thought, if all else fails, I'll extract the information I need from this dumb shit taking a leak. But there was no way he survived that steel door bouncing off the back of his head at a thousand feet per second. The sheer pressure from the roof hatch dropping blew every door and window off the building, wired or not.

Access was granted. Even before the flames died back we were on the move. Don and John entered from different points but both from the north and I from the east. This way we would be initially aware of each other's position to avoid getting caught by crossfire. Chris flew in and landed on the solid portion of the roof near the stairwell. She was in before the first shot was fired, her timing impeccable. These idiots didn't know what hit them. But the few guys left to stir were no strangers to combat invasion, idiots or not.

"John. To the right," Don yelled.

John quick fired two rounds center mass into the first torso he saw, shoved a steel rack out of his way and rolled to a cover point beside another.

Don was hit in the chest by the butt of a weapon and knocked back as he held the trigger on his auto, lighting up the shop. Eating bullets, his assailant went down hard, hitting his head against the carbon body of a glider. Don threw himself down next to him for cover and the sides of the craft lit up with a blue hue and a reverberating hum. He pulled two grenades with his left hand, popped the pins with his mouth and dumped them into the glider as it accelerated out through the blown door. One hundred yards out of the building and the glider exploded into a massive fireball accentuated by the dark night.

I went through the kitchen exchanging fire from a grate platform at the top of an expanded metal staircase. I had to be careful and allow room for Chris to descend the stairwell. The guy on the platform turned to look up, startled, and his head rocked back, flipping his body over the handrail to the racking below.

"What do you see, Chris?" I snapped.

"You've got two just to your left in the couches. I'm going to clear the top."

She fired a few rounds into the sofa area for tracking and moved out of the open. I threw a flash grenade to blind them and dove to the side to get a shot off. I caught a round to my chest, knocking me back as I unloaded. It felt like I was struck with a sledge hammer but nothing penetrated the Kevlar blanketing my vitals. One of the two gunmen went down and the other scrambled behind the bar. I could see his reflection in the broken TV on the floor and knew he could see me. I loaded another magazine as I shouted.

"I'll make you a deal. Tell me how to find Dillon and I'll let you walk away from this."

"Fuck you," was his response.

I holstered the nine and slipped my sawed-off from its sling, destroying the bar with three rapid fire double-ought rounds. He ran and Superman-dove behind the kitchen bar cabinets as I grazed him with shot from the fourth.

Gunfire was echoing through the building. I could tell Chris was engaged on the upper tier and I looked over while John sliced a guy's throat without hesitation. *If I needed one alive, this might be my guy.*

"I just want to talk," I yelled to him.

"Yeah. I see the way you talk," he said.

Debris was everywhere from the destruction caused by the retractable roof. Half the interior was crushed under the panels, leaving a massive hole and exposing the sky. Smoke and haze filled the air, making it difficult to breathe or see. I slung the shotgun and wrapped my hands around what was left of a wooden bar stool. Holding it over my head I kicked a piece of dislodged floor tile towards his barricade. He popped up and I hurled the stool over the counter with enough force to break bones. It shattered over his bulk, disorienting him and causing a misfire of his weapon. I capitalized and was over the counter in a flash, targeting his gun. With short crisp movements I slammed his arm to the marble edging, breaking it free, and came up with the back of my elbow connecting with his chin, feeling his teeth crack on impact. I proceeded with a couple of body shots, dropping him to the ground. Recovering in a blink he caught my right leg as my boot made contact and took out my left ankle with a wooden spindle from the stool. I went down hard and unexpected on my shoulder and took a few more unanswered blows to the body. He was swinging like Bamm-Bamm and had the strength of a plow horse. I drove my bootheel into his knee, folding his leg backwards, and came up with the other splintered stool leg, piercing his chest just under the sternum. I let go and stepped back, allowing his body to fall to the floor, driving the stake clean through. *So much for words.*

Don and John were clearing the bottom floor, going room to room and leaving death in their wake.

Don. We need answers," I said. "I'm heading up. You got this?"

"Got it," he said, drowning out with gunfire.

Chris had one last room to check, Dillon's master suite and office was still intact just off the garage platform overlooking the newly exposed shop below with a clear shot of the overcast night sky above. A couple of hovercraft gliders sat on the edge outside the room. One of them teetering the jagged hole in the floor, ready to plummet. Chris walked by and gave it a shove with her foot and watched it flip over the edge and smash into the iron slab below with a satisfying crunch of carbon and metal. She kept her gun drawn and approached the door. When she reached out for the lever the door flew open with velocity, knocking her back as Grant barged out like a locomotive. His shoulder struck her side as large arms wrapped around with an iron grip. She was helpless. He picked her up off her feet and drove to the wall, removing the air from her lungs and bouncing her brain off the inside of her skull, turning the lights out within. Grant threw her body to the ground like a rag doll and jumped into the remaining glider. The vibration shook off dust and debris as it came to life, propelling Grant like a rocket through the open roof.

I fired a couple of futile rounds at the fleeing glider from the top of the stairs as it accelerated out of sight. Chris moved her head with a slight shake, trying to regain some clarity.

"Go get him, Ken," she mumbled.

Using the handrails I took the stairwell to the roof four steps at a time and flew through the blown door like Superman. *It's time to put my Ducati to the test.* Leaving the top down I donned my helmet and accelerated to over 250 MPH. He was in my sight in a matter of minutes. Grant was flying low to the ground, trying to use the rocks as cover. He saw me approaching fast in the distance and wove through a sawtooth formation of red and orange rock illuminated by our lights. I followed suit, gaining with each maneuver. Clipping corners with the glider's magnetic field I bumped his side and fired at his power source. The unique carbon fiber shell of his glider reflected the bullets at this speed. I needed to slow him down but didn't quite know how. All I could think of was the energy launcher Dillon had demonstrated. I pushed slightly ahead of him and forced his glider to turn back in the direction of the shop, then maneuvered behind for guidance.

Chris slid back into action and peered down at John who was grappling with a monster of equal size. John had the strength and determination of ten men on the battlefield yet was struggling with his adversary. The Goliath had John from behind in a chokehold but John tucked his chin down and was not giving it up. He pushed back with his entire core, driving Goliath against an open plasma cutter. Chris had no clear shot and needed to get down to ground level to be of use, so she headed back to the stairs leading down to the demolished kitchen.

John threw his head back into the Goliath's jaw and felt the grip seat under his own chin. Mistake. He knew he would be out in a matter of seconds. He slid his left hand along the platform's edge and found a toggle switch. Praying that a program was set he flipped the switch up and felt the vibration of life. His ears were pierced from the instant screams of Goliath as the vise on his neck broke. John dove forward as flames shot from the man's chest in the shape of a D\M. John grabbed the lid and slammed it down, covering the burning body so it could fry in peace. Chris rounded the corner with her gun raised just in time to see the man's legs give their final involuntary kick.

John and Chris looked at each other as the last shot rang and silence ensued. Don came through on the mic. "East clear, two live. Whatcha got?"

They assessed the damage briefly. "All dead over here, sorry," John said and grinned sheepishly at Chris.

"Don, you there?" I asked.

"Affirmative, all's clear. Got a couple of live ones, let that guy go and come back," Don said.

Grant retracted his top and pointed his handgun. I knew at this low altitude I would be susceptible, so I curved up on my side, exposing the bottom shell of the glider to take less damage. I rolled over the top of him and bumped from the other side then reversed the move. It was like bullying a younger sibling. Having the speed advantage allowed me to keep him flying low and heading in the right direction. We would be over the shop in minutes.

"Can't let him go, Don, don't want him alerting Dillon." *If he hasn't done so already.* "Look around the shop and see if you can find one of those energy launchers they had."

"Found a few of them. John's playing with one right now."

"Well, get it to the roof. I'm bringing this guy home."

"Ten-four."
Rocks flew back like buckshot, showering my glider as he clipped every outcropping he could find. I put the shield up and gave my all to bump him out of the rock formation to open ground. He pulled up fast to try and shake me. I elevated like lightning, nosing down from above, forcing him to drop once more. He hit one last outcropping, crumbling a large chunk of red rock to the valley bed as we burst to open sky in direct line with the shop.

"Don, how we looking? We're coming in fast from the north. About two mics out," I said.

I bumped him once more from the top and briefly made eye contact. He was clearly frustrated and had given up on the gun.

"In position, Ken, bring her home," Don said.

As soon as we were within firing range I pulled up out of the way and yelled, "Clear."

Don had him locked and fired the round with pinpoint accuracy. Grant panicked as he lost power and descended towards the roof with zero control. His glider struck the south end of the roof, taking out a section of the pony-wall perimeter. Brick rained to the ground as he crashed, churning up earth and scrap before a junk pile of heaping metal objects stopped his momentum. I brought the Batmobile down next to him and swung my shotgun into the wrecked pod, pointing at an empty seat. He must have ejected or scrambled out on impact. I squatted down between the gliders and listened for a moment. Don and John came out of the building with Chris, guns drawn.

"Get down," I said. "He's out here somewhere."

I motioned for Chris and John to spread out and come in from the sides. Don knelt down next to me.

"Let him go, Ken, we've got two in the shop," he said.

Before I could respond, shots fired. Don grabbed his chest from the side and dropped forward to the dirt. I pulled him up and pushed his back against the Ducati as blood soaked out the side of his vest.

"Oh no, Don," I said, pulling his tactical gear off to assess the severity. *Oh shit.* "Hold on, buddy, hold on... Don's been hit." "Where did it come from, Ken?" John asked.

"Somewhere over by that trailer," I said, applying pressure to Don's chest.

A crack from a high-powered rifle echoed off the distant rocks, causing my nerves to contract, tucking me tighter to my barricade.

Grant stumbled out from behind the trailer and fell to his knees holding his mid-section. John moved in fast when he saw the weakened man. Grant raised his hand to take aim and John struck it with a shotgun golf swing, knocking the pistol from his grip, and put his combat boot square to his throat, dropping him to his back like a sack of potatoes.

"Hold him, John," I screamed. "Just hold him. Chris, get over here quick, keep the pressure here," I said and replaced my hand with hers. "I have to go deal with this asshole before John kills him… Hang in there, Don. You're going to be all right." *You're going to be all right*; I thought and ruffled his hair.

As I approached John three figures came from the rocks towards us. I spotted Walt with his rifle in hand.

"Nice shot, my friend," I said.

"Thought you might want him alive for a bit," he replied.

"I don't even know how you saw him out here, Walt."

"Your eyes get used to the dark. Sometimes you can see with better clarity at night than you can during the day, especially with old, sensitive eyes."

"Well, my eyes are still young. Drag his ass to the light, John," I said.

John grabbed him by the neck and gave a boot to the gut, flipped him over and dragged him face down by his feet, like a caveman with his prize.

"That was quite a show you just put on there, Mr. Ken," Walt said as we followed.

"Glad you enjoyed, thanks for the help."

Now it was time for business. I took possession of Grant and looked around the half shop, half rubble before me.

"Clear that vise, John," I said pointing with a head nod. "And Walt, help me out here."

It was a large, solid iron vise, with a cross crank slide rod for leverage. It was mounted to a stout workbench that was anchored to the concrete at its feet. *Perfect.* For quick results you couldn't get much better.

Walt helped me place Grant's head into the vise face up. I cranked it tight until his body hung on its own and took a step back.

"Hey, John? Why don't you bring those other two assholes out here so they can watch. I doubt they know what this guy does, but just in case," I said.

Walt was like a kid in a candy shop.

"I like your style," he said with an ear to ear rotten smile, like the homicidal switch was just flipped.

"Glad you approve. Now let's get this started. Would you like to do the honors?" I said and pointed to the vise with an open hand.

"Does a horse piss where he pleases?" he said and grabbed hold of the crank, drawing the slide into position.

I zip-tied Grant's hands behind his back while I spoke. "Let's start with your name there, fuckface."

I paused and got no response so I threw a power punch to his rib cage, feeling ribs crack on impact, then nodded to Walt and watched him apply pressure to the crank.

John pushed the other captives to their knees for the show and knocked both their heads with the shotgun for good measure.

"Are you really going to try and hold out on me?" I said with surprise in my voice. "You are going to die. That I can guarantee. You answer my questions and I'll put a bullet in your head and end your misery. If you don't, I will break every rib in your body and move on, leaving Walt here to slowly crush your skull over the next couple of hours."

"I vote for you to keep your mouth shut. This is fun," Walt added.

I grabbed a large machine bolt about an inch in diameter from the counter and made a tight fist with it seated securely in my palm. I pulled a greasy shop towel taut over my knuckles and pinned it between thumb and forefinger. He began to talk.

"Grant. My name is Grant," he said.

"Good decision," I said. "I'm looking for a girl, about five foot seven, blond, blue eyes… This ring a bell there, Grant? The one you put your filthy fucking hands on and took from the elevator at the Hilton?"

"She's with Dillon on his boat."

"What boat? Where?"

"I don't know the coordinates."

I slammed my fist down feeling ribs crack and glanced at Walt. He turned the crank a little more, keeping the pressure. Grant's eyes opened, bulging with a glossy red lightning bolt pattern. Sweat beaded out of his head like clear blood as he tried to scream and express his pain with lungs that would not permit it.

"Satisfy me, Grant. I need more," I said.
"It's called The Claiborne. It's somewhere off the coast of Florida… Fort Lauderdale area. They move around a lot to stay off the radar. That's all I know. Now please," he pleaded.

"What kind of boat, Grant?" he started to fade for a second. "Stay with me now, what are we looking at… big… small… how many on the crew?"

Grant hesitated. I threw my fist like an impact hammer to the same spot, crunching bone and flesh.

"Big one, mega yacht… two or three hundred feet… about fifteen on the crew."

Fluid was coming out of his nose, mouth and eyes, mixing with blood and sweat. His legs were giving out and his neck was folding back unnaturally like it was about to snap.

"Are you ready for that bullet now, Grant?" I said and motioned for Walt to step aside. I brought the hammer down once again, bursting organs.

Before Grant could spit out a please, I reared back and kicked hard, sending my bootheel into the crank shaft. I could hear his skull pop as his face caved in and his neck snapped from the weight of a limp, lifeless body. Blood, matter and other life fluids oozed out over the vise and down his neck and torso like lava. "There's your bullet, bitch," I whispered and turned my attention to the others.

I pulled my nine and looked at the terror on the faces of the two young men flex-cuffed on their shaking knees before me.

"Any ideas on how to find this Claiborne, gentlemen?" I said.

They continued to shake with fear and stared at me with unblinking eyes, but a cat had their tongues. So I put a bullet in each head and moved on. Enough time had been spent here. Don needed help fast and I needed to find The Claiborne. The clock was ticking and I knew just who to call.

# Chapter Fifteen

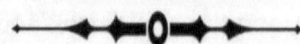

James Detrick awoke to angry birds with a mild hangover. He opened the wood louvers and smiled at the sight of Janet's naked body leaning on the handrail. Forty feet below was the Gulf of Mexico. It was going to be a beautiful day, calm waters after a rough storm, God's therapeutic gift.

The cell phone vibrated against the glass top of the nightstand next to an oversized digital clock reading 5:30 AM.

"Hell…" was all James got out before he was cut off.

"Dad. We're coming in. Be there in thirty," was all he heard.

"What? If you want me to be hospitable, you're not getting off to a very good start."

"Sorry, tried calling a couple of times. Got a situation here, pops. Lucy is missing and Don caught a bullet. It's all fubar. Fill you in when I get there. Can you get hold of that redhead, Janet? You said you were still seeing her."

"Looking at her right now," he said with a smile.
"Have her get some medical supplies, we're gonna have to dig out a bullet."

"Take him to a hospital, Ken."

"Don doesn't like hospitals and we're short on time. I'll explain everything, I promise. Hey, I'm gonna need your help on this one, Dad."

"Door's open, Kenny. Just get here."

\*\*\*\*\*

The storm had died down in the vast Atlantic and the morning sun assaulted their eyes. It was a long night for Dillon and his crew. And an even longer night for Lucy and the non-stop nightmare she was living. Dillon and Jax met in the lounge for a drink before they retired for some slumber.

"Good job, Jackson. Did you give them a ceremony?" Dillon asked.

"A gangster's ceremony… Couple of words over the drop zone."

"He was a good man. But this is still a time for celebration, Jax. And I want the guys in good spirits."

Jax mixed up a couple of stiff whiskey and Cokes.

"Cleaning up that kind of a mess doesn't really put you in a good state of mind, Dillon. We could have used the shark tank on Joe and your point still would have come across, you know."

"It was less a statement and more of a reaction. Besides, that's what they get paid for. I'll make it up to them tomorrow; I'm having some girls flown in for the night. Jamie's coming with some goods and everyone's getting a bonus for the work on the launcher."

"Nice, that will boost some morale," Jax said with a drawl and handed Dillon his crystal to make a toast. "To $1.2 billion… un-fucking-believable."

"It's a beautiful thing, my friend."

"Dillon, let me ask you something. It's been on my mind. What's it like being linked with the girl? I mean… how does it work?"

"Holy crap, it's unreal, I should have done it a long time ago. It's a constant game, carnal, raw, with mass emotions. Feeling her fear is something totally new to me. It's difficult to describe."

"Try."

"Well. It's a knowing fear. It's like being five again and having your father bust the bedroom door off its hinges. Then that moment of sickness you feel at the sight of the studded belt in his hand as the light flickers off the stones imbedded in the buckle.

But the feeling doesn't go away. It just blends. Like a perfect melody of emotions."

"So what's it like when you do her? Can you feel her get off?"

"You're getting a little personal now, Jax."

"Yeah, whatever, just answer the question."

"I haven't fucked her yet."
"What? That's the first thing I would have done. That's one fine piece of…"

"Well, we all have our fetishes. In due time there, Jax."

"I think I want to try it… Neuralink."

"I'll tell you what. Let's talk about it when we get back to the states."

"When are we heading out?"

"Couple of days. We'll kick the boys to Sedona, stop by Shafter's for supplies and get the hell out of Dodge before this weather quits being so kind. You ready to work on your tan?"

"Hell, yeah," Jax said and finished his drink. "Life is good, my man."

"And it's the good life that makes death so sweet."

"You're a sick motherfucker, Dillon. Another?"

Dillon slid his glass towards Jax with his index finger in a point. "Load her up."

As they drank, the topic of conversation took a turn. Dillon was a different kind of man and Jax had learned to read him. He knew when to steer clear and when to pry. They discussed the tripod mounts and how Dillon was pleased with the outcome. Tomorrow they would test them out. Then they discussed the crew. First, who would be the best gunners under duress. Ray had proven himself in California and earned a spot on The Claiborne crew. Tommy had done an efficient and flawless job running the disposal mission and earned himself a spot as well. Isaiah had apprehended Lucy quickly and seemed to know his way around the ship, earning a promotion to captain, and would make a fine replacement for Tony and Joe, whom Dillon had blamed for the mishap.

*****

The hovercraft and gliders flew down to the Detrick landing pad off the top floor in short order. It was a three-story, wood-sided home, with hunter green steel roofing overlooking the naval ship yard. It was a small place with steep staircases, soft pastel colors and panoramic views.

James and Janet met the crew on the landing pad and helped get Don into a spare room they had set up for the task at hand. Janet knew what she was doing and took over. She was professional and efficient and had done her entire career in the medical field with some of the best hands in the world, and it showed. The bullet in Don was a fragment. It must have ricocheted off a piece of metal in the scrap yard before striking Don. If it was a direct hit it would have exited his body clean. Janet retrieved the partial bullet through a small incision in Don's back. Two more inches and it would have been out on its own. No vitals were struck and internal bleeding was minimal. She had him stitched up in no time and he was taking a little morphine nap while we filled in Pops on the entire situation.

"So you work for this Portman guy?" James asked Chris.

"Yes, sir," she said without elaborating.

He kept his eyes trained on me.
"So let me get this straight. Right now your crew consists of you, one and a half fishermen and a bikini model?" The sarcasm was heavy.

"Don't underestimate them. You should see what's left of Dillon's shop in Sedona," I said.

"Well, first thing we do is find out where this Claiborne is, and exactly what we're dealing with."

"You got any ideas on that?"

"Yeah, he's called the Proctor. If anyone can find this guy it's him."

"Well, let's get the ball rolling."

"I'll get the ball rolling. You guys get some rest. A couple of hours will go a long way. I'll make some calls and see what I can do about beefing up your crew some."

We took turns showering. Then Janet gave us each a half tab of Ambien and tucked us in like we were children. All I needed was some warm milk and a fluffed pillow.

*****

As the sky warmed and the sea calmed, Dillon retreated to his room to close his eyes. But before he would succumb to his needed slumber, he would check on Lucy once more. She had been moved to the master suite and restrained in the cell after a thorough cleaning of Enriquez's and Tony's remains. Flashbacks entered her mind as she looked up through the open doorway to the familiar bath. Dillon gave the room a white glove once more and shook the visions from his own mind.

"How are you feeling, baby doll?" he said in a tired, gravelly voice. His body was worn from the highs and lows. The drugs and the travels of the day, as well as the alcohol had taken their toll.

Tears flowed from Lucy's eyes uncontrollably as she rolled her head down to her shoulder and buried her face. Dillon knelt down beside her and wiped her tears with the back of his finger like a loving father to his daughter. For a second she thought his personality had flipped. Then he moaned sexually and licked the salty tears from his finger. Lucy turned her head to the other side as he put his rough hand between her thighs and pushed his coarse wet finger upon her, probing, violating every essence of her being.

"I know… It's tough being angry while you're stimulated, isn't it? You can't hide it, Lucy," he said. He pulled his hand up over her breast to her mouth and made her suck his finger clean. This was the first time he had touched her sexually. And she knew resistance would prove futile.

"We're going to have a lot of fun on this trip, baby. Do you want something to help you sleep?" he asked.

She shook her head and whimpered, "No, Dillon, please don't."

He rolled out the hype kit and fixed her a bump. *The hook.* "This will get you started, nothing too heavy." He loaded her up and shared in her virgin taste. It was like he was young again. That amount would have been useless if not for the link.

Dillon left her alone and sprawled out on his silk sheets. Loaded his syringe with the good stuff and hit the bloodstream hot. He lay petrified, staring at the ceiling, and would not move for hours. *Let's dream a little dream, Lucy, let's dream.*

*****

"Get up, sunshine," James whispered, shaking my shoulder.

I rolled over and blinked heavy eyelids.

"How long was I out?"

"About five hours. Don't wake the others. Let's go, the Proctor's got some information for us. We're going to meet him at Flyer's in about ten. You'll have to buy him a beer. That's the way he works."

I freshened up a bit, thinking of Lucy, remembering the dream we had shared, her smile, the warmth of her lips. I fought back the tears and met my father at the top of the stairs. He took me in his arms as I could no longer contain my emotions. For a full two minutes I wept on his shoulder as he embraced me. He was my rock and I felt his pain as he felt mine. We broke with no words exchanged. None were needed.

A short ride in my new glider put us at the platform of Flyer's diner, the best greasy spoon in all of Pensacola. The Proctor was waiting at a table in the back, away from the dying lunch crowd. He rose to his feet for our introduction.

"Ken, meet Admiral Sheldon," James said.

I shook hands with the Proctor's iron grip. It made me think of the vise I used to pop Grant's head mere hours before.

"It's a pleasure. I've heard a lot about you," I said.

"Likewise. Have a seat," he said, ending the cordialness.

He snapped his fingers at the waitress, drawing her attention to the table. She appeared like Dracula changing from bat form and filled the air between my seat and the Proctor's.

"What can I getcha?" she asked and gave her bubble gum a pop, audibly reminding me of Grant once more.

"We just need something to wet the whistle, hon. A pitcher of Sierra and three frosty mugs will do. Thank you, doll," the Proctor said, taking control of the table once more.

She nodded her head like Genie and poof.

"What do ya got for us?" James said as the waitress vanished.

"My guy recommends Shafter's," the Admiral said without missing a beat.

"What the hell is a Shafter's?" I asked.

"That's right, you're a California boy. It's the largest fuel station in the Atlantic, basically a floating city that these large ships can dock to. They have everything you can think of, supplies, maintenance, lodging, entertainment, bars, everything but real estate."

James chimed in, "Named after Thomas Shafter, the inventor of a polystyrene foam/concrete combination slab. They link these things together with some kind of an indestructible expansion joint for movement. Then anchor to the sea floor with a cable system that can move up and down with the tides. It's pretty incredible."

"And why do you think we can find Dillon on one of these islands," I asked.

"Because The Claiborne is not on the list for the milk run," he said.

"You got me. What the hell is a milk run?"

"Basically these yachts like The Claiborne take on too much damage during hurricane season, so they have to tuck tail and run. You have two choices, take the three-week voyage across the Atlantic yourself, or pay for the milk run. Most yacht owners choose the latter. There are a couple of outfits that provide this service. The main one is out of Port Antigua in the Windward Islands of the Caribbean. They have extremely large vessels that can fill their hull with water, trek in twenty to thirty of these mega yachts at a time, strap 'em down, then drain the hull for the run to the Mediterranean. The other outfit went under this year -- no pun intended -- and Antigua does not have The Claiborne on their roster."

"Does that explain Shafter's? How do you know he hasn't put on the burners?"

"I know, my sources say that he has yet to hit Shafter's for the necessary maintenance and the supplies that would be required for a trek of this magnitude. Shafter's is the last stop and he only has a few days left before he has to get the heck out of Dodge."

"Good, nice work. So tell me more about this Shafter's. What's the security like, can we hit The Claiborne from there?"

"Security is tight and they're not going to be interested in our situation, trust me. I have a man in position looking out for our friends and I've made arrangements for a room close to the docks for surveillance purposes. But the hit will have to take place in open water, outside the secured perimeter of Shafter's."

"What about infiltrating when they dock? Maintenance staff maybe?"

The waitress appeared with pitcher in hand and filled frost covered mugs as we sat in silence. It wasn't until she disappeared that the conversation resumed.

"No possibility. Like I said, security is tight. There is no way you're boarding that ship at Shafter's. Just wait until they get out to sea and it's game-on. That brings up another thought. This guy Maxwell is the one that merged with Portman Industries? Is that correct?" he said and downed half his mug.

"That's the one."

"Portman is a tough S.O.B. Is he or any of his men involved with this Claiborne?"

I shrugged my shoulders indicating that I didn't have a clue. I could tell that made him uneasy. He didn't want any part of Portman Industries. We all drank for a second, not really enjoying our beers.

"Look," I said, holding out my hands. "I don't think so. Besides, Portman isn't as tough as you think. He was strong-armed into that merger somehow by Maxwell and he thinks he was Neuralinked and manipulated into signing that contract. But one thing is for certain, Dillon will have the EL40 on that ship; food for thought."

"Okay, look guys," James said, sounding just like Ken. "First thing we've got to do is get a look at this yacht and try to work up some schematics, and Sheldon, see if you can't talk to your guy and figure out a way to get a tracking device on The

Claiborne. I don't want him getting away from us. I've got Miller and Woody going along for the ride and I think we all need to get our eyes on that ship to know what we're dealing with. What do the accommodations look like at Shafter's?"

"Plenty of space, it's a flat and it's ready to go, sleeping arrangements won't be a problem. Move out any time, the sooner the better," the Proctor said.

We finished the pitcher off, left a tip for She-racula and parted to round up the troops. Next stop was the so-called infamous Shafter's.

# Chapter Sixteen

The hall was dark and wet, lined with iron cell fronts. Had it been lighter the musky smell might have been a tangible vision. Each cell was slightly illuminated but from where, Lucy could not tell. She lifted her head, glanced down and saw buckled leather straps securing her to a rusted medical gurney. All she heard was squeaky wheels and the periodic grind of metal on metal when they rubbed. A large bulky shadow of a man pushed her along the corridor in silence, amplifying the sounds of hell.

Lucy thought she was in a dream. *This must be why I can't feel my body*, she thought, then remembered the needle -- Dillon's needle -- and the feeling of hot heroin entering her bloodstream like molasses. *Is this a dream or the drugs? Are you there, Dillon? Are you there*? She thought she heard his low raspy laugh. More like a fast hum of laughter. But it was off in the distance yet in her head, vibrating her eardrums from far yet within.

A face slammed against a cell front. A face streamed with tears through grime, exposing the bruises of man. The young girl cried out with a haunting moan. Lucy turned her head to look away and another young captive's face hit the cell front on the opposing side. It struck the bars like she had been thrown from the back of the cell. Blood spilt from her forehead as she tried to scream through bloody duct tape. "Where am I? What are you doing with me?" Lucy screamed at the shadow man. The laughter returned from within, then echoed to the infinite distance.

The shadow man did not respond. He just kept pushing at a slow, relentless pace from one cell to the next. Faces continued to come forward as if she was the freak show to be seen and taunted. People, animals, alive, dead, undead, each cell produced a scene of horror; a young boy that looked as if he had never seen the light of day and would never know what it was like to smile; a dead wolf with foam bubbling out of its mouth, muzzle stuck in a vicious snarl; a muscle-bound shark thrashing in the cell, blood and slime flying, scarred and cracked flesh slamming against the bars, breaking the rusted bolts from the concrete anchors.

Lucy could not make sense of the random images. This had to be Dillon interjecting. She decided to fight back and searched her past for strong, clear memories. Her thoughts manifested in the cells, replacing Dillon's nightmares. Her father throwing the football; her childhood dog, Dobie the beagle, jumps at the bars to play. *It's working, this is working*, she thought. But Dillon responded quick and strong, casting images into the cells with hers, snuffing them out violently before her eyes. Vicious wild animals, ruthless mutant psychopathic killers entered and destroyed, reducing Lucy to tears and submission. Then came the dark laughter.

The intensity of the dream had Lucy in a pool of sweat. She pried her eyes open and begged for reality. But was that wise? She was stuck in an unimaginable dark place.

Her mouth was dry and her tongue was swollen. Getting to her feet was not an option right then, as her body was fatigued from God knows what. She pulled her torso over the rim of the toilet and lapped some water with her tongue. She felt like burying her face and drowning out of this world. Then Ken entered her mind and she realized there was still a little smile in her soul. Something worth living for. Worth *fighting* for.

*****

We flew out to Shafter's following my father's lead. Enormous would be an understatement. How I had never heard of this place was baffling. But with the technological advances of today, many things escaped my attention. It was the size of Kauai but completely flat. Towers, lights, modern architecture and jagged docks made Shafter's resemble an alien spacecraft resting on our ocean.

There was very little air traffic at the time, making our approach uncomfortable. I felt that our train of hovercrafts might draw unneeded attention. We just needed to land before The Claiborne docked. We rounded Shafter's massive red and yellow logo mounted on top of what appeared to be the tallest structure on the island. I wondered if Shafter himself was in the penthouse. If the island was a spaceship, this building was clearly the command center, at over one hundred stories tall.

A smaller version of the building sat just off the docks and donned the name Stella's. Stella's roof opened up with plenty of clearance for our group. When the last craft was in, the roof closed and the walls illuminated with horizontal rows of neon. The floors were marked out like an advanced runway to direct our flight. With a digital floor grid our route was customized for our party and easily navigated. The high ceilings and lack of vertical supports were eerie. Suspended were small shuttles like ski lifts hanging from magnetic channels. They disappeared, engulfed by glowing tunnels at the end of the run. We powered down in the designated stations and quickly grouped up to do our ooing and ahhing. This place was extremely clean compared to anything on the mainland, virtually dust-free. Extra-terrestrial? Maybe. Artificial intelligence? Definitely.

"This is incredible," I said to no one in particular, looking around the space-age parking accommodations.

"Yeah, yeah, grab your bags, our ride is here," said the Proctor, pointing to the ceiling.

The shuttle pods emerged from the grid above and hovered behind our crafts. The floor marked out the loading zone and directed us under time restraints. We quickly strapped in, not knowing what would happen if we faltered on the time. Each pod held four passengers plus luggage with ample room. We sat in silence as the pod moved at remarkable speeds, slowed down, dropped vertically and resumed. This went on for several minutes as we descended to our level. With one final drop we were left at an entry point to a long, spacious hall.

Multiple elevators and pod loading zones lined the end of the corridor. The Proctor set off on foot with purpose and we followed suit. The hall was fashionably lit with modern sconces that gave a slight homey feel despite the color assault of the commercial flooring. Ten floors above the water we entered a flat two times larger than my home on the beach, which I longed for.

I immediately noticed the view of the main docks below through the panoramic, floor-to-ceiling glass.

"Wow. This is going to be perfect," I said, again to no one in particular. I hooked my pack on a chair and headed to the terrace for a better look. The Proctor was on his phone and stepped out behind me as he terminated the call.

"Still no sign, we slipped in," he said.

"Good. What time are your boys supposed to be here?" I asked.

"Any minute now. No worries, you're in good hands."

We looked down at half a dozen mega yachts and daydreamed. I had money but this was sick money. This made Miami look middle class. Most of the yachts were already headed to the Caribbean for the milk run. These were the diehards here. The Proctor explained that the trip across the Atlantic was hard on the ships. The salt water was damaging and a thorough cleaning before and after was necessary. They would seal the decks, handrails and any exposed wood, buff every inch of chrome to a shine and scrub down the hull above water and below. This could take weeks. He doubted The Claiborne was in very good shape considering it was the last boat to visit Shafter's, showing a lack of care in preserving its functionality and beauty.

*****

"Rise and shine, sleepyhead. The sun's going down," Dillon said to Lucy, pulling her to her feet. She was light, but little help in her rag doll state. "Come on, baby; let's get you in the shower."

The shower had been rigged with eye bolts that he fastened her restraints to, hanging her naked body against the cold, unforgiving marble. The shower head pulled from the wall with an extension hose. Dillon put the water to her flesh and used his rough, bare hands to lather her youthful body.

Lucy flinched at his touch. "Warmer," she muttered… "Please."

Dillon warmed the water up a bit and enjoyed rubbing on her and feeling her utter disgust at the same time. He produced a straight razor from his pocket and pressed it against her soapy wet ear.

"Are you enjoying this?" he said, putting his lips to her other ear. "Say yes or it gets bloody."

"Yes," she whispered, without the energy or position for defiance.

Satisfied with the response, he dragged the blade down slow, gliding over her throat and chest, barely cutting the surface of her skin. A few droplets of blood found their way to oxygen, leaving a trail of iron scent in the soap. Dillon thrived on the smell of her clean body and fresh blood. Taking deep breaths through his nose, he shaved the stubble from her armpits. Examining her body closely he scraped off any peach fuzz or unwanted hair that shimmered in the light. He pulled her legs apart and shaved her clean as the day she was born. After a good rinse he dried every inch of her body using a soft towel with a sensitive blotting motion, thriving on her disdain.

"There you go, baby, a work of art. Did you enjoy your little dream earlier?" he said with a beyond-creepy tone.

She shook her head as he retrieved a bag full of perfumes and lined them on the shower ledge.

"You have a strong mind, Lucy. I'm impressed. You are turning out to be quite the catch," he said. Dillon paused for a moment in contemplation, looking at the different perfume bottles. "My mother used to collect. What's your favorite, Lucy?" he asked.

"Let me guess... Curve... No... Daisy... I'll tell you what. Let's start with a Fougere; reminds me of fluorescent green ferns, fresh and clean, urban style. My favorite, Liz Claiborne, mmm..." He sprayed her neck and arms, watching her wince at the sting of the cut. "Now, a little Chypre; the island scent goes well with Claiborne. You will like it." He sprayed the flesh of her belly and legs generously and put his bottles back in the leather satchel. His movements were meticulous, like each bottle was a precious heirloom to be handled with the utmost care. Lucy was floored by how a tough Neanderthal like Dillon could be such a pussy. But she knew he could crack at any time. So she suppressed her true thoughts, but relished knowing he felt the mockery.

"I'll fetch you some clothes and take you to see my baby when I get back," Dillon said and walked out of the room, leaving her alone and exposed and feeling like a feeble lamb.

\*\*\*\*\*

James poked his head out. "Come on in, guys," he said. "Ken, this is Wood and Miller. They're going to help out and Woody here has got the floor."

"Great, nice to meet you gentlemen," I said, and shook hands. "What do ya got for us?"

"Well, let's have a seat, we have quite a bit to go over," Wood said.

The few standing obliged, getting comfortable around the great room while Don proceeded to set up surveillance equipment covering the docks. But his ears were on. They were always on.

"Don't mind me," he said. "I'm listening."

Heads nodded around the room.

"You know what? Let's go ahead and start with you, Miller. Tell us what you found out on this Claiborne," Wood said. It was clear this was not the first time they had worked together.

"The Claiborne came from a Swedish yacht manufacturer in the late 1900s and was originally named the Greta, which is Swedish for The Pearl. Obviously it has been renovated several times since then. The latest modifications noted were completed by a Viking Yachts Builders out of Anacortes, Washington. I have made contact with a rep from Viking and am currently awaiting schematics from the renovation." He typed into a link-pad as he spoke. "The original prints are no longer available but he archived some of his preliminary sketches of the layout and details of the modifications. He's tracking down and scanning as we speak."

"So what do you mean by modification?" I asked, losing patience.

"As soon as the link comes, you will understand," Miller said. "But I will tell you this; it was some very unorthodox stuff for a yacht builder. Like converting a section of the servant's quarters into iron cells, putting in restraint systems. Most of the suite was overhauled, engine work, landing aid. But the strangest part was the conversion of the pool to a 425,000-gallon shark tank with a six-inch-thick plexi top. In order to do this he had to collaborate with a marine biologist from the University of California. The guy's name is Sean Plunket. He specializes in this kind of stuff apparently. You want to take it from here, Woody?" We turned our attention to Wood as Don calibrated one of the scopes.

"Well, what's interesting about it is that it is highly illegal, but apparently money talks. About ten years ago Dillon purchased a fifteen foot great white that was scheduled for release. This shark had spent most of its life in captivity and Sean felt comfortable with the deal. Well, his pocketbook felt comfortable, anyway. We're talking a three-hundred-pound, slate grey killing machine. With three hundred serrated, flesh shredding teeth. These suckers can sense a tiny amount of blood up to three miles away and it's confined, gentlemen. Not to mention that it is on the endangered species list. This is a predatory animal we are dealing with. Sean said if it hasn't had a substantial meal within the last two months, you could be it."

"In other words, don't do the backstroke with it," Don said, setting up a monitor just inside the terrace.

"Exactly," Wood said. "That's a given, but it's good to know potential hazards. There is one good thing about our little sharky friend… He's been tagged for observation." "What does that tell us?" Chris asked.

"He has a tracking device on him and Sean's getting me the code. Originally it was used to study navigational patterns as well as keep track of the population. There are less than one hundred adult males within the state's waters. This device is web based and mobile. It's on a ninety second loop tracking GPS coordinates. If he's still on that boat, which I bet he is, we'll have Dillon in the palm of our hand."

"I have a question," John said.

"Shoot, big guy," Wood said.

"You said a substantial meal. What do you mean by substantial?" John said with a quizzical look.

"Well, a small meal would be fish or rays. A larger or a more substantial meal could consist of other sharks, small harbor seals, sea turtles, or a human." John swallowed loudly, not liking what he heard. "I need a drink."

Dillon met Jax on the upper deck to inspect the launchers and try out a few rounds.

"The mounts are functional and very stable, which will aid with accuracy," Jax said.

"Is the weather going to be a problem?" Dillon asked.

"We can disconnect from the mounts, install hard cases or just keep them well-oiled and leave them be. They will hold up."

"Keep 'em oiled. I want these puppies ready at all times."
"No problem."

Dillon grabbed the paddles and swung the EL40 one hundred and eighty degrees and back to get a feel for the motion.

"Nice... smooth but tight." He rapid fired two rounds off into the distant waters. "Feels good, let's check out the other one."

They worked their way to the back of the boat with a little pep in their step. Life was good despite the bumps.

"As soon as we're done here I want you to get Isaiah and have him meet us at the tank. I want to feed Barron," Dillon said. "Lucy will be joining us. She'll get a kick out of him and maybe she will think twice about trying to escape again."

"Sure thing... Isaiah said they just picked up a small seal before we got here and he's been holding it for you."

"Perfect."

Lucy knew she was in pain but felt numb. Her hands were discolored from the pressure and her shoulders were on the verge of dislocation. Dillon marched in and gave her a slow, animalistic sniff as he fondled and pinched at her left nipple, undoubtedly feeling as if his actions were seductive. He removed her wrists from the ratchets and dropped her to her knees on the hard shower floor. Lucy collapsed to her back as Dillon exited the dank shower.

"Your clothes are on the toilet, and hurry up; I have something to show you, and Lucy... don't be stupid," he said, propping the door open.

Lucy looked up at the shower head and knew that there was an extension tube concealed within the wall. *Don't be stupid*, she thought and crawled to the bathroom floor. She took inventory of her surroundings. A thin pants and shirt combo, like transparent pajamas, is all she found.

"No panties or shoes, Dillon?" she said softly.

"We won't be gone long, now let's go."

She obediently got dressed and came out of the bathroom with her arms crossed over her chest and her head down. Dillon pried her hands apart, showing his slow, controlled, strength. She was no match in her condition. He cuffed her hands behind her back and pushed her towards the door.

"Let's go, cupcake, clock's tickin'," he said.

# Chapter Seventeen

Chris's phone buzzed. She glanced at the screen and quickly muted the sound and excused herself from the flat.

"Holy fuck. Do you not have any patience?" Chris snapped as she rounded the corner and went through a door labeled Community Garden.

"Let's not forget who pays the wage here, young lady," Alex responded.

"I told you I would call when I could."

"Just fill me in. What the fuck is taking so long?"

"We've figured out a way to track them, but it's easier said than done. They are on a yacht heading out of the country as we speak. And I almost got my ass blown off back in Sedona, thanks for asking."

"Give me a timeframe at least."

"Fuck you, Alex. Let me do my job and don't call me again. I'll be in touch," she said and terminated the call.

"Who was that?" Don asked as she turned.

Her adrenaline jumped. His large frame blocked her path.

"My mother," she said.

"Your mother's name is Alex?"

"If you knew who it was, why did you ask?"

"To see if you would lie. And you did. What did he want?"

"He just wants me back in Vegas, that's all. Wondering what's up."

"That guy seems like a real penis. How come you didn't introduce us at the fights that night? Considering he paid for the seats, it was kind of awkward."

"He didn't give a shit who sat in those seats, Don. And he doesn't like to meet new people."

"I call bullshit. I have a feeling he already knew who the seats were for."

"I did tell him ahead of time, but trust me, it didn't make a difference."

Don stared at Chris for a few seconds, then looked off in the distance at the docks.

"We should head back and stay together," he said, stepping to the side.

Chris nodded in agreement, breaking the tension and lead the way back in silence.

*****

Dillon prodded Lucy along and pushed her through the door to the tank room. Lucy stopped short of the glass floor like a stubborn mule.

"Oh-no-no-darling," he said, "all the way to the middle." He forced her out over the water and jumped up and down a couple of times as they moved. "See? No worries, it's solid. Light her up, Jax."

The lights around the perimeter of the tank came on, casting a clean white light evenly throughout the tank. The shark came up directly under their feet, startling Lucy.

"Holy shit," she screamed and started back the way they came.

"Hold on," Dillon said, grabbing her just above the elbow. "Meet Barron, my pride and joy."

"I don't want to."

"Oh, come on. He's lonely. He needs some company."

Barron swam back around and came up under Lucy, bumping the plexi panel she was on. She stood frozen as chills riddled her body, making Dillon smile.

"Isaiah," Dillon shouted.

"God speed, little guy," Isaiah said, and released the feed tank, dropping the seal to Barron's domain.

Lucy saw the seal swim straight up and smack against the glass, trapped, with nowhere to hide, nowhere to jump. Barron locked in and accelerated. The world's most deadly predator chomped down on the seal, killing it instantly. A blood cloud swirled as Barron consumed the seal in one gulp, spinning his muscular body and tail fin through the blood cloud, dissipating the crimson water, leaving no sign of the helpless harbor seal.

"Ye-he-yes," Dillon shouted, took his grip off of Lucy and raised his arms in victory, like a child. "That was awesome."

Lucy was sick to her stomach and Dillon knew it. His grin said it all. Barron came up and hit the panel below Dillon as if asking for more. He got down and put his hand on the glass.

"Not today, buddy. We like to keep him hungry in case, well, you know," he said to Lucy.

Lucy's body shivered at the thought of a human being gruesomely consumed by the great white.

"Can we go now?" she asked and looked Dillon in the eyes for an answer.

"Jax, take Lucy back to the room and give her a little something to calm her nerves," Dillon said. "I've got to check on Jamie. She should be here any time now with our party package. Isaiah. Thank you. Shut her down."

*****

"Here we go," said Miller, bringing up the file from Viking Builders.

The drawings formed in the air over the bar counter in a flat, two dimensional picture.

"Not bad for preliminary. Spread the layers out so we can see the levels," I said, very impressed by what I was seeing.

Everyone gathered around Miller seated at the bar as he navigated the drawings with a laser pointer and gave a narrative of the markings.

"The lower deck mostly consists of guest cabins with some servant quarters. This row here has been converted to cells, accessible here and here. This is an elevator but it's not clear whether it accommodates all levels. They could be stacked."

"How many levels are there?" James asked.

"Looks like five. But the upper deck is only the captain's quarters and the bridge with a small exterior platform."

"Where is the shark tank?" John asked, with uneasiness in his voice.

Miller snickered at John's discomfort.

"Looks like it's here, labeled as the sun deck. But it's actually indoors. This portion here," he said, pointing, "was converted for a hovercraft labeled as a hauler, probably quite large. Just inside these doors appears to be a gym and Jacuzzi area and here is your infamous shark tank."

John made a funny sound of disgust.

"And this would be a pump room," Miller continued. "Here is the feeding tank, electrical chase, ventilation… a pretty elaborate system. No expense was spared here. I would assume they don't have to keep the tank balanced. They just continuously cycle the water out with the ocean like they do on cruise ships. Looks like the same type of filtration."

"What's all this?" James asked, pointing to a mess of scratches and mathematical figures.

"That's pretty much just a dock for crafts. Gliders, boats, etc. This stuff here is some kind of laser-assisted landing device. It targets your craft and guides it in. Would come in real handy in inclement weather," Miller said.

"Okay, tell me about the meat and potatoes. The main deck," I said.

"The main deck consists of a grand entrance, the owner's suite forward, a state room, more than likely for a bodyguard, and a bar and ballroom. And this is a small dining area just above the kitchen."

"You had said they overhauled the owner's suite. Do you have those details, maybe a sectional?" I asked.

"Yep, we've got sectionals on the cells, the tank, and the owner's suite. Not much on the landing pad for some reason."

"Let's see the suite," I said.

My stomach turned as a three dimensional sectional image appeared before us. A restraint system on the bed and seating areas was mapped out. The master bath showed the eye bolts in the shower and in the cell. Thoughts of Lucy strapped to that wall brought on a world of emotions that I wouldn't wish upon my worst enemy.

James interjected to get Miller to switch the image.

"Let's just layer it back together please. Are there any details on weapons?"

Miller layered the drawings back to two dimensional and shook his head.

"I don't see anything that looks like weapons. But these are yacht builders. I'm surprised they did all this. Plus this was over a decade ago. Who knows what they've done since then."
"Hmmm… Good point," James said.

"We've got a beacon. It's a faint one. But like a pregnancy test, that's all you need," Wood said from behind us.

"We've got coordinates? Where is this son of a bitch?" I said.

"I don't know yet. It's all oceans to me. Let me map it and draw out the satellite."

It took Woody a matter of seconds to work his magic. I couldn't believe how close we were, thanks to these guys. I could only cross my fingers that Lucy was still alive.

"Looks like they are close, half a day maybe, by morning they'll be here," Woody said.

I got down to business. "Keep an eye on it, let me know if they change course. Miller, bring up that landing pad again. We need to know if there's enough room to land or if we need to make room. We need to mark out all the stairwells, screw the elevators. We also need distances, the most efficient routes to the electrical and engine rooms and note where we might need explosives. Dissect and memorize these plans, gentlemen, I want control of this ship before my soles hit that deck."

"We're going to have a small window when they get here. It's going to be a quick in and out, fuel and supplies only. By midmorning they will be gone," Wood said.

"Be ready to go at any time. When they're here I want an idea of how many are on the crew, do they have an arsenal on deck and how many hovercrafts. We need room. As soon as they get out of Shafter's waters we hit 'em," I said with certainty.

*****

Dillon, Jax, Ray and Tommy stood on the landing pad as Jamie's craft was guided in. A large man of muscle with the look of a casino boss stepped out first and gave a helping hand as Jamie exited the craft. Dillon had Ray and Tommy escort the young men and women who followed to the ballroom. Six beautiful ladies, a couple of guys that looked like secret service agents to go along with the casino boss, and a D.J. with equipment in tow. Dillon put his hands together and rubbed vigorously as they made their exit.

"What do ya got? What do ya got?" he said to Jamie.

"The usual times four," she said.

"Good, because we have a long trip ahead of us. You really outdid yourself this time, Jamie. The girls are top notch, you came through on the package. I don't know how to thank you. I just want to give you a big hug."

"Don't touch me, Dillon. You're still a fuckin' freak." "For old times?" he asked with his arms out.

"Yeah right, not a chance. You can show your appreciation with greenbacks."

"That's what I love about you. Straight shooter," Dillon said, pulling an envelope from his breast pocket. "Something a little extra for you, darling."

"Well, thank you," she said, quickly snapping it from his hand and feeling the weight with satisfaction. "Now don't forget, those girls need tips, Dillon. And I need not say… no rough play… right?"

"No problem, doll, don't bite the hand that feeds you, got it."

She nodded and handed him the package. "I've got to go, duty calls," she said and stepped back into the craft and gave the pilot the thumbs up. The craft rose with a hum as the door lowered. "Remember, eight AM sharp at Shafter's."

"Got it," he said and blew his long-time friend a kiss, and she was gone.

The crew was waiting anxiously in the ballroom, already a little liquored up. They could hardly contain themselves when the girls walked in. Beautiful girls, a variety of flavors strolled in, put their bags against the wall and took a seat on the closest lap they could find. Tommy went to the bar and set up the muscle with their drink of choice while Ray helped to get the D.J. on track. Within short order the party was blowing full steam.

The bass line kicked as Dillon and Jax entered the room. A couple of the girls left their prospects and greeted them like kingpins. Dillon embraced with a little fondling and sent them back to the crew. This was their night.

"Listen up," Dillon shouted and gestured for the D.J. to temporarily tone the volume down. Ears and eyes were immediately attentive. "Jax will be handing each of you an envelope. This envelope contains your party money for tonight. I expect… all of it to be in the hands of these lovely ladies by morning. Your bonuses will be wired. A hundred thousand apiece for a job well done… Party up, gentlemen."

The music rhythmically returned, the crew raised beverages and the ladies exchanged smiles. While Jax was divvying out funds, Dillon proceeded to set up a smorgasbord of drugs on an oval glass table in the center of a plush, half oval, white leather bench seat. A mound of cocaine -- soon to be destroyed -- made up the centerpiece.

They partied late into the night. The girls were dutiful and professional, keeping their wits about them. But the crew of The Claiborne cut loose, over-drank and over-indulged with narcotics. When they felt like fighting they took it out on each other instead of the girls, as they were instructed by an extremely hypocritical Dillon. But it was his show and no one wanted to see his wrath on one of their own.

Shitfaced and feeling the room spin, Dillon decided to go see his Lucy. He stumbled into the bathroom and slammed the door open to Lucy's cell. She shifted back against the wall in disgust as Dillon, breathing hard, dropped himself down on top of her, straddling her body and slowly began to grind himself against her chest. Lucy's body was still in a relaxed state but her mind was returning. Dillon was obviously inebriated and she thought this might be her best chance, maybe her only chance.

"You like that, baby?" she said with seduction. "Tell me you like it."

"Oh, baby, I like it, mmm."

Lucy bit down on his growing manhood through his jeans, teasing him. She heard his breathing become rhythmic as she gnawed seductively. "Do you want me to suck on him, baby? Take him deep?"

"Oh, God yes."

"You want me to swallow it or show you, baby?" "Oh God," he said, ripping his belt open.

"Uncuff me, baby. Let's go to the bed. You can tie me to the posts like you want to and I can do this right like a porn star," she said, trying to keep her mind clear of her intentions.

He hesitated for a second then sat back on her legs, fumbling for the cuff key. She licked her lips staring into his glossy eyes and held his gaze.

Lucy tried to keep her glare seductive but visions entered her mind. Flashes like a dream distracted her. Dillon's state made his mind weak and Lucy realized that he was not controlling his thoughts like before. She was seeing his mind flow like a drunkard's tongue. An image of Dillon's hands flashed holding her head down on him. She could feel her body convulsing and her lungs struggling for air. His hairy flesh flashed inches from her eyes as she choked and gagged uncontrollably.

He pulled her free of the cuffs and dragged her to the door.

"Wait, Dillon. I have to pee," she said, pulling back from his grasp.

He let her go and sat down in the doorway, leaning his head back on the doorjamb as he watched her squat to urinate. The room was rotating like a carousel as he tried to read her thoughts to no avail. His eyes closed for a second and Lucy sprung. Throwing the shower door open, she pulled the shower head out of the wall, drawing the tubing to the max, placed her feet on the wall and yanked, breaking the threaded connection. Dillon rose to his feet and made an attempt to charge, but he was stopped cold by a whipping blow to the head. She held tight to the hose and swung the shower head again and again, like a medieval flail. With blood running into his eyes, he reached up blind and caught the hose, pulling her down with it. Lucy let go but fell into him, kicking and thrashing. He rolled on top of her, blinking the blood from his eyes. She took advantage and connected an up-kick to his jaw, rocking his already pounding head back hard against the wall. She broke for the door but Dillon was two steps behind her. Walls of blood flashed in her head, thick, dripping, partially coagulated blood. She stumbled over the bed and grabbed the sliding door handle as Dillon's body drove her into the glass. She spun around and threw a knee to the groin and an elbow to the face. Blood smeared across the dual pane like Passover. He came back hard with a punch to the throat, knocking Lucy back towards the bar.

Dillon's foot kicked hard into Lucy's chest as he gained back a fraction of sobriety, following through with a right cross. Pain shot to her core as he turned relentless. He was going to make her pay. Adrenaline coursed as he picked her up by the arms and swung her around horizontally over the bar. She crashed into the glass shelves, shattering bottles and glasses with her body. She fell to the floor on the edge of consciousness. Glass cut into her palms and knees as she pushed up with all her might. Dillon came around the bar and Lucy used all she had left in her to drive a fifth of Crown like a baseball bat into his left knee. He collapsed to the tile but reached out, pulling himself on top of Lucy amidst the shards and liquor. Bloody and wet, he slipped one arm around her neck and got his other hand on the back of her head. His legs wrapped around her body from the back and she felt him synch in the choke.

With no more strength to fight, she was asleep within seconds.

Dillon loosened the grip as her body went limp. Breathing heavy from exhaustion, his brain spun. *Why the fuck did I take her restraints off? How stupid can I be? Never again, Lucy, never.*

## Chapter Eighteen

Dillon looked like the walking dead that next morning and he was still harboring an extreme amount of anger, some towards Lucy but mostly himself. She was not an ordinary woman and it excited him in a way. She was strong and determined... But it was time to break her down. Beating her would not do the trick. She had already endured more than most men could handle and her mind was proving to be stronger than expected.

"Oh my Lord, what the hell happened, Dillon?" Jax said upon seeing his battered head. "You look like you got chewed up and spit out."

"Good morning. Nice to see you too," Dillon said. "Listen, Jax, I'm going to need you to handle the details at Shafter's this morning. I'm going to be occupied for a bit."

"No problem, consider it done. Did Lucy do this?"

"I might have overreacted in taking out Joe. This girl is no joke. I fucked up and took her cuffs off last night."

"Oh man, are we going to need to do a drop?"

"No, I didn't kill her, but it's lesson time. Have Isaiah meet me in the state room, I'm going to need his assistance."

*****

Lucy was in and out of consciousness and had no concept of time. She didn't know how long she had been missing. Was Ken searching for her? Did they have the memory card she had dropped in the elevator that day? Questions faded in and out of her frontal lobe like an unforgiving tide. A dark cloud descended over Lucy, gripping her core with a pure unmovable fear. Something in her last episode of defiance had changed Dillon. She had seen his sick, twisted mind from the inside and had witnessed his lack of remorse and his carnal brutality firsthand. And the fear of knowing, without a doubt, that the monster was beneath the bed made her pray for deliverance.

Lucy was cuffed to the cables again in the state room where Dillon had brutally slain Sheila. Images of Sheila's battered corpse filled her vision when she looked at the empty chair that had been wiped clean of her blood. She looked around the room, taking in her surroundings. There were several restraint systems throughout, a large white leather sofa, a single camera on a tripod and a large video monitor. Everything was cold and clinically clean. She looked down at her body and noticed that she had been cleaned as well. The glass shards had been removed from her wounds, bandages and wraps were applied with the technique of a professional and an IV pumped a clean saline solution into her veins. The realization that Dillon was keeping her alive for the time being just intensified her fear.

Bam. Every pore on her body jumped as the door slid open hard and Isaiah rolled in a filthy, drug-enslaved Rebecca.

"Straight from the bowels of the boat, one beautiful young Rebecca, delivered for your viewing pleasure," Isaiah said.

Lucy tried to speak and plea out to Isaiah, but her mouth would not open as it was sealed by a perfectly cut rectangle of Gorilla tape from cheek to cheek.

"Mmm!" Lucy screamed.

She watched Isaiah hook Rebecca in and tape her mouth shut with presumably the same tape that bound her own speech.

When Isaiah left the room pushing an empty wheelchair, Lucy fell apart. Tears flowed uncontrollably at the thought of what was to come.

"I'm sorry, I'm sorry," Lucy mumbled under the tape. *I'm so sorry.*

\*\*\*\*\*

A short time later Isaiah returned with Carmen, stopping Lucy's tears. She could not believe what was transpiring.

"One more to join the party, the beautiful Ms. Carmen," he said.

Isaiah hooked Carmen into an adjacent system, pulling her arms up hard to raise her torso and giving her a kiss before applying the tape.

"You were always my favorite," he whispered in her ear.

"Mmmmmm," Lucy pleaded one last time.

Isaiah stopped and looked Lucy in the eyes with discontent. As if to say 'This is your fault,' but took a slightly different route. "My favorite verse as a child read that 'the way of man seems right, but at the end of it, is the way of death.' And you have entered into a death-link. God speed, Lucy."

Isaiah wiped his hands as to say 'I'm clean' and exited the room. Dillon waited until the doorway was clear. And like a man under hypnosis, slid in like a snake with a predatory, glossed over gaze. Lucy immediately hung her head and the tears flowed.

*****

Isaiah took control of The Claiborne as they approached Shafter's.

"Nice timing," said Jax by his side. "Looks like we are the last of the yachts. Cutting it close, don't you think?"

"Nah, we've got plenty of time. The rest are just a bunch of pansies," Isaiah said with an 'I got this' confidence.

"Well, I hope you're right. Supplies should be waiting at the docks and fueling should only take about an hour, right?"

"You need to relax, Jax."

"I know. Dillon just wasn't himself this morning. He's got all the money in the world and he's fucking around with this Lucy while we're pulling into Shafter's. He thinks he's invincible sometimes. Like the world revolves around him."

"His switch definitely flipped. You should have seen him standing outside the door as I brought the girls in. He just stared out to sea like he was counting whitecaps. Gave me the chills."

"Well, I hope he gets this shit out of his system. Or it's going to be a long trip. I've got to head down and see the girls off. See you in a few."

*****

Jax met some of the crew down on the main deck as The Claiborne passed the Shafter's marquee. The letters were thirty feet tall, cascading over the entrance to a massive marina. The guys always liked it when they docked here. It was like a weekend pass for NAVY boys. But this time it was strictly business. They had their orders and knew they were under time constraints.

"As soon as we get loaded he wants you guys to head back to Sedona," Jax said to the group. "But I'm going to need some volunteers to hang back for a bit. We might need some clean up and disposal soon."

"He's off the hook, Jax," one of them said. Jax looked around at the men.

"If you can't stand the heat, get out. Go back to Sedona and enjoy your bonuses. But you keep your mouths shut, understood?" Jax said sternly. "If you want to earn some bones, raise your hand."

Some heads bowed and some hands rose. Jax had his crew.

*****

"Should be entering the marina any time now, guys," Woody announced, watching the tracker.

"Got 'em," Don said.

The Claiborne appeared on the monitor, perfectly gliding through the water like a friend of the sea. Ken's heart skipped, knowing better.

Everyone got into position to get their eyes on the mysterious Claiborne. She was a beauty from a distance, top of her class at one time. As she approached, the neglect became more prominent. Polished chrome letters spelling *The Claiborne* trimmed the hull. This was apparently the only polished piece on the yacht. The teak rails had lost luster and showed signs of dry rot, the decking looked as if it could splinter and the windows were salt blown.

"Damn, what a piece of work," John said.

"John, get a count on the crew," I said. "Dad, map out the decks. I want to know hovercrafts, artillery, everything." "Are those women?" Chris said.

"Looks like gals to me," John said.

"Any of them Lucy?" I asked. "We need to be sure in case she tries to slip the boat.

"I think they are escorts, no sign of Lucy," Don said.

"Yeah, they must be guests, they're preparing to get off. Some have bags. Hey, there's that guy from Vegas," John said.

"Definitely," I said, as my blood boiled. "He was with Dillon at the demo."

Knowing that Lucy could be on that boat was killing me. I wanted to act now and all could sense it.

"Calm down, Ken. Take a breath. In due time, Son," James said as I paced the room with clenched fists.

I went back to the scope and peered hard as The Claiborne docked, looking at each crew member's face carefully; still no sign of Lucy or Dillon.

"Check out the hardware," someone said.

I then focused on an EL40 mounted on a tripod swivel with dual spade-handled butterfly triggers. This made the wheels spin.

"Dual triggers, take one arm out, it can't be fired," I said.

"Nice to know," responded Woody with a head nod.

Adjacent to the EL40 was a fifty caliber M2 Browning machine gun mounted on its own tripod, giving it about a two thousand-meter range. It could probably throw eight to nine hundred rounds per minute. Good thing was it had the same type of trigger system as the launcher. *No worries from the drummer of Def Leppard.* I swung the scope to the rear where they had the same set up, a fifty cal with a forty millimeter launcher.

"Hey, Ken?" Miller called. "It looks like some of the crew might be leaving us. They're loading up one of the hovercrafts."

"Chris, keep an eye on that for me. Make sure Lucy or Dillon aren't on that craft," I said.

"Sure thing," she said and turned her sight.

The girls left the boat and the crew loaded the supplies under the watchful eyes of Shafter's security staff. I got the feeling that this yacht often brought trouble. Nevertheless, they were clients. After about thirty minutes we had what we needed and started brainstorming.

"As soon as they leave we should load up. It will take 'em about twenty minutes to get out of Shafter's water. And let's give them another twenty to be clear. We can't afford any interference or give them a chance to hook back around, Shafter's security teams patrol the water constantly," the Proctor said.

Miller took over, "Look, no one is manning those guns. The threat is not there. It looks like they had a long night partying and are up early against their will."

"Don't underestimate them. We can't take any chances with those guns, Miller," I said. "We've got to take them out first, despite appearances."

"I agree, if we drop from high enough we might get a clean entry, secure the bridge and rig the guns without any detection at all."

"Looks like that craft is taking off. I counted six, still no sign of Lucy or Dillon, though," Chris said.

"Good," I said. "Less fuckers we have to kill."

We spent the next half hour going over the plans. Systematically we would have the yacht covered within minutes of boarding. Things were going to happen fast. Just a short wait longer. If all went as planned, Lucy would be in my arms in no time and Dillon would be fighting for his seat in hell.

Against the better judgment of my crew, myself included, I decided to take a quick stroll down to the docks rather than pace the flat like a caged cat. I had to give it a shot. See if I could make contact with a member from last night's Claiborne festivities. The docks were busy with lots of movement, yet I felt as if all eyes were on me. A short brisk walk from the base of Stella's put me at the gates. There appeared to be only two ways in. Both were heavily guarded and required member passes for access in and out. Public access was segregated and enforced by waterway patrols and the restricting shape of Shafter's docks.

"You won't get in there, so don't bother trying," a voice said from behind. "You may as well walk around."

I turned to see a young man with a tackle box and rod in hand. The kid seemed harmless, yet savvy.

"What's the closest I can get to that big boat out there without drawing too much attention?" I asked.

"I'll show you but if they catch you spying you had better play dumb," he said and gestured for me to follow.

He led me through a labyrinth of small buildings to the base of a tower. I made mental notes to backtrack the route.

"This one is vacant right now," the boy said, referring to the tower. "But the eyes are always on you so don't be fooled. You can walk up to the fence there," he continued, pointing, "but that is as far as you'll get, my friend."

The boy continued walking as if we were not together. *Survivor,* I thought.

"Thanks," I said as he vanished as stealthily as he came.

I walked along the wrought iron fence as if I was out for a Sunday stroll. I spotted a waiting area just inside the fence and noticed stainless cases under the awning, the same cases that came off The Claiborne. A girl sat a little farther down as if deep in thought.

"Psst," I said, trying to draw her attention.

She had short red hair, a thin neck line and lazy body language. Her fishnet stockings were torn and by far the nicest part of the ensemble. She looked in my direction and cocked her head to the side like a puppy.

"Can I ask you a question?" I said in a non-threatening voice.

"Sure, what can I do for you, hon?" she said and slowly chewed what appeared to be gum. Couldn't tell, might have been a tick.

"Did you come off the big boat there?"

"That's the one, sweet cheeks."

A large bearded face blocked my view suddenly.

"Fuck off," the beard blurted.

I stepped back out of reflex but kept my cool.

"I just had a question, sir," I said.

"Where she came from is none of your business."

"Listen, I know you guys came off that boat. I just need to know if you saw a girl, or heard about a girl that might be held captive aboard?"

The beard pulled on a cigar and leaned into the fence blowing smoke from his oversized nostrils.

"That boat is a client, and a good one at that. They pay well and are decent to the girls. Rule number one, don't rat out a client. Now like I said, fuck off."

I lunged my arm through the fence slats and grabbed the back of his neck and jerked his head forward. His face smashed between the iron, blackening both eyes. The last bit of smoke in his lungs leaked out as his lips quivered through the scraggly beard.

"Answer the question," I demanded as I pressed the barrel of my nine to his sternum, holding his fat face to the fence.

A light shock pulsed through my arm, biting enough to cause me to let go. Beard jumped back, grabbing at his face as the cigar hit the dock at his feet.

"What do we have here?" a security guard said as he approached, dragging a cattle prong from rung to rung, creating sparks for effect.

I realized that I had let the situation get out of hand and needed to make an exit.

"Sorry, sir, just leaving," I said and took two steps back.

"Run along now," the guard said, then mumbled something into his mic.

I picked up my pace as I rounded the tower and quickly realized the severity of my error. Shafter's security force closed in on me like Secret Service on a White House breach. I was disarmed and restrained in a carrier within seconds of contact.

A man stepped in within two minutes and took the seat opposite of my own. His blue eyes were drilling and demanding of no bullshit. I knew that my crew had witnessed the apprehension and were probably running in circles. But they had been advised to stay put no matter what.

Without introduction, blue eyes cut to the chase.

"Listen, dipshit. We know about you and your little surveillance party you've got going on. We know you've had your eyes on The Claiborne since she entered our waters. But here's the thing. What you do within the confines of your suite is your business. We have plenty of peeping toms around here. No biggy.

But when you start harassing our bread and butter well, that's a whole 'nother story, and I can guarantee that you and your crew will be removed from the equation by the hand of my staff." He stared, letting the thought linger.

"I meant no disrespect but this a matter of life and death," I responded.

"It is always a matter of life and death. I don't know what your situation is, nor do I care. As a matter of fact, I get paid not to care, Mr. Detrick."

Hearing blue-eyes speak my name hit home. I saved my breath and nodded my head in understanding.

"Two miles, Mr. Detrick. That's how far our waters stretch. If you so much as breathe on that boat within our water, you and your crew will be shot down, judge and jury. Is that understood?"

"Yes sir, sorry sir," I said. This man held a position that lacked morals yet commanded respect, and that I admired.

"According to my calculations you have about ninety minutes before The Claiborne is in international waters. So I suspect you will be checking out soon," he said and winked a blue eye as he handed my nine millimeter back, dangling it from his forefinger.

I holstered the gun, feeling slightly embarrassed of my actions as the doors slid open exposing the lobby of Stella's. I stepped out and felt the wind at my back. I didn't notice the wind before but I had a strange feeling that luck was on my side.

# Chapter Nineteen

We left Shafter's with pure adrenaline coursing through our veins. Miller had the beacon and would orchestrate the drop time. We stayed high -- at about 30,000 feet -- and approached The Claiborne from behind. Even if detected by radar, at this altitude we would be inconspicuous. I had my fingers crossed that these idiots were hung over and went straight back to sleep, letting their guard down. The captain might be the only one to eye us. But from a vertical approach that was unlikely.

Chris killed the power on Miller's signal and popped the cargo door to Portman's hovercraft. Miller gave a count from five and we were gone. Woody and I barrel rolled for effect, got our bearings and gave each other a thumbs up while the rest of the crew cleared out before circling back. I would normally have enjoyed the rush and relished in the silence but my mind was consumed with the mission. With Lucy. It was time for them to pay.

The Claiborne was invisible for the first 10,000 feet. We nosedived for speed as soon as it came into view. Point of entry was just behind the bridge in the control cabin. It might be vacant and on autopilot by this time but we couldn't count on it.

There was one guy lying on the bench seat in the control cabin as I hit. It was all I could do to touch down softly and reel my chute in. But Woody was a pro. He did a double arm pull to one hand and on the touch and rise, pulled a sig with a silencer and put a round through the back of the guy's head. From dreams to the gates of hell, the schmuck never knew what hit him. Woody quickly had his chute in <u>while</u> I was still tucking. We didn't want to release and give something more to be noticed. The doorbell would ring soon enough.

We separated without a word and headed for the guns. One hundred and twenty seconds later, as scheduled, I located the unmanned assembly and packed a small amount of C-4 explosives into each weapons tripod, right at the top. Too much could blow the front and back off the ship. We wanted to stay afloat long enough to find Lucy and get the hell out safely. Any other energy launchers that we came across would be locked away in Davey Jones' locker before we made our exit.

Satisfied with my rigging I headed quietly but swiftly to the sun deck in search of the hauler. Woody headed to the back dock to rig the gliders and watercrafts. Nobody was getting off this ship unless I said so.

I approached the hauler from the front. Easily found with no guard to be seen. Cab was clear. All directions clear and eerily quiet. I swung around from the side and unlatched the rear cargo doors. With a pull, the muzzle of my shotgun led the way. The hauler was clear of flesh but packed with steel, a mobile armory. This was too easy. I packed the hauler and rigged the door with the last of my C-4 within my timeframe. Woody would no doubt be done on schedule. As I cleared the corridor of the sun deck I uttered my first words since the drop.

"Brace... three, two, one."

Boom. Boom. Boom. Boom.

The ship rocked as fire entered the sky, signaling my crew and theirs. *Let the games begin.*

*****

Dillon slammed the door open and held his back to the jamb, staring into the sky. His clothes and arms were blood covered as he pulled the latex from his sweaty hands. *Portman*, he thought. *That son of a bitch. Who does he think he is?* He ran to his room to don what gear he could find. Most of their weapons were in the hauler and judging by the explosions were disintegrated.

Woody laid down cover fire so our crew could land while I went straight for the owner's suite. The crafts swung around and landed with ease and the team was out covering their routes as I popped Dillon's blood smeared slider. The room was eerie and smelled of death. The bar had been broken up and blood was splattered throughout the suite. I feared the worst as I slowly rounded the corner into the bathroom with my gun at the ready. Blood painted the floor and cabinets, accentuating the gruesome scene before me.

Peeking into the cell I took a hard blow to the side of my head, forcing me into the shower door as it exploded into a thousand tempered pieces. Dillon was on me like a wild animal. He rammed the butt of a shotgun down on me like he was spearing a mammoth, connecting with my head and again to my chest. The lights faded for a moment and Dillon ripped the gun from my fingers, putting the barrel of his shotgun to my eye socket.

"You working for Portman, mother fucker?" he said.

I responded by whipping my head to the side and driving a palm to the barrel, bringing my boot up into his rib cage, knocking him back. I hung onto the shotgun and he pulled the trigger, rocketing lead into the shower, ricocheting off the marble, spraying my back and arms.

\*\*\*\*\*

Miller held the docks and protected the crafts while Woody and the Proctor headed down to clear the lower level and rig the engine room. James took the upper deck and engaged in gunfire, immediately dropping two of Dillon's men. Don and John went to the main deck and Chris to the sun deck. Gunfire echoed through the yacht on every level, turning the walls into Swiss cheese.

Separating, Don took the left and John the right. As they approached the ballroom, one on each side and entering in opposite corners, they directed their bullets at a diagonal to stay out of crossfire. The room was cleared in less than thirty seconds, leaving four bodies and a riddled interior.

Don and John worked in sync. Very little communication was needed between them. A few hand signals here and there moved them about. They ascended a stairwell and John knew the shark tank was just ahead. He hesitated slightly, forcing Don to take the lead.

Isaiah was lying in wait and just as Don cracked the door he aimed the handheld sonic weapon in their direction and pulled the trigger.

*****

Woody covered the floor while the Proctor loaded the engine room with clay. The drum of the machines and distant gunfire filled their ears. The Proctor found the fuselage and gave his partner the thumbs up. He wired four full bricks to the seam and one to the head. As he exited the engine room he looked at Woody to give a nod and noticed a forlorn look on his face. Woody's eyes looked down, drawing his sight to an empty cell. Blood and filth made them both cringe. They looked from cell to cell, thankfully finding no one captive. The chills they felt solidified their desire to dispose of this vessel and its crew. The Proctor pointed to Woody, gesturing to move out.

"Lower clear," Woody said to his mic.

"Upper clear," James followed.

*****

Dillon's body went back as I drove my shoulder like a bulldozer into his gut. We hit the door jamb and spun into the room, crashing down in the seating area. Our weapons were free as neither of us wanted the other dead just yet. He wanted answers and I needed to know where Lucy was. Plus I badly needed the satisfaction of beating Dillon within inches of his life with my bare hands.

I came down hard with my elbow, breaking his nose and adding to the blood on his shirt. A couple of dropped hammer fists to drive the pain to his core and he flipped in retreat. I landed a solid hook punch to the side of his battered face before he rolled again. He came up with a chunk of marble from the broken coffee table, connecting with my jaw. I didn't see it coming. I rolled to the side of the bed and Dillon caught me with a hard kidney punch, packing the buckshot as if he were tenderizing a steak. I swung with a backhand, driving the edge of my fist into his windpipe. As we got to our feet he grabbed me with a vise-like grip and churned his legs toward the slider. Our combined bulk blew through the glass like it wasn't there. I hit the rail backwards and flipped over as Dillon extended his arms in a final push. Helplessly I cartwheeled over a lifeboat and grabbed an old rope with one hand. Burning the flesh from my palm I let go and slapped the water with my back. The last thing I saw was Dillon's brimstone eyes and blood-lined grin looking down with satisfaction.

Out of pure instinct I stroked aggressively towards the boat and grabbed hold of the back dock, swung a foot into the ladder rung and called out to Miller.

"Jesus Christ, Ken. What the hell happened?" Miller said as he pulled me aboard. "We're doing like twenty knots. That was insane."

"Well, it wasn't a leisure swim. That guy is a beast. He's much bigger up close and strong as an ox."

"Top and bottom are clear. No word from the other decks," Miller said as I traded out my vest and repacked.

"Hold tight, Miller, be ready to go," I said. Gave him a nod and moved out.

*****

The sound gun was usually used to keep Barron at bay. But when discharged under the water the sonic waves are somewhat interrupted. To a 3,000-pound shark it was just annoying. But to a 240-pound man, above water, the impact would be much more severe. At about two hundred decibels, the high powered sonic waves knocked Don and John's equilibrium off and toppled them to the decking. Their eyes vibrated in their sockets, causing a temporary blindness as their central nervous systems rattled to the point of severe pain and disorientation. Don was completely incapacitated and John felt nauseous as blood dripped from both eardrums.

Tommy grabbed Don and dragged him inside the door, sliding him face down over the glass floor. Isaiah stepped in while Tommy went to grab the other guy. Isaiah held the retract button on the control panel, retracting a large section of the glass floor right next to Don.

"Come on over, Barron. I've got something for you, baby," Isaiah said.

Tommy reached down to get hold of John but this one was not as affected by the sound waves and had regained his footing. John came up fast and hard, headbutted Tommy like a wrecking ball, caving the bridge of his nose and bouncing his front teeth off of his vocal cords. He threw a solid body shot to the liver before he could orient himself and heaved him over the railing to the cold Atlantic.

Don pushed up on all fours, squeezing his eyelids together. Isaiah stood over him, drew a serrated blade and dragged it across Don's gut, ripping the flesh open. With a boot to the side of his body he rolled him over the edge of the glass, creating a bloody splash. John busted through the door and put a round into Isaiah's chest, blowing him back into the water, and quickly dove, sliding face first towards the edge and reaching his arms out for his brother.

Isaiah grabbed onto Don and pulled them both in while reaching up and driving his knife into John's side. John roared as Isaiah twisted the blade. Don broke free and frantically went for air. Barron made a stealth circle underneath them and John looked down in sheer panic and pain at the sight of blood draining from his body as a bloodthirsty great white targeted in. He shoved a chunk of explosives, pre-wired with a remote detonator, into Isaiah's jacket and shoved him under with his legs. Pushing him between himself and Barron as the massive jaws opened to receive his meal. Barron clamped down on Isaiah and spun, pulling the knife free and dragging his entire body down into the depths of the tank. Don grabbed his brother and pulled him to the edge of the glass, pulling himself out, never losing his grip on John. Once John's torso was up he gripped John's legs, rolling him completely out of the water. They both looked through the glass as John mustered the strength to pull out the detonator and hit the switch. Barron's head exploded in all directions, creating a large crimson mess of limbs, fragments of flesh and undoubtedly razor sharp teeth swirling in a cloud of blood and matter. The glass floor started cracking in sections as Don slid his brother out through the door, feeling him dying from within.

"John. Don't do it. Don't you die on me," Don yelled as he held him in his arms, pushing on the gaping wound. Blood poured out around his hands. Tears welled in his eyes as he felt John's body gasp for air. Blood gurgled and ran from his mouth, mixed with bubbles and strings of saliva. "Please John, please," he cried as he felt his brother go limp and a piece of his own inner core slip from this world.

John's eyes were glossed over and vacant. Don ran his hand over his brother's face, seeing a mirrored image of himself, closed his lifeless eyes and wept uncontrollably as he tended to his own wounds.

*****

Jax fired a barrage of lead into a couple of lifeboats, dropping one to the water.

"I know you're in there, bitch," he yelled.

Chris dove down into the middle of four boats and worked her way to the end.

Jax lit up another, annihilating the old tattered boat and showering the ocean with wooden fragments.

Chris was panicking. She had no way out and did not want to die this way. *Bold and brave*, she told herself and returned fire as she leaped back over the rail at the end of the run and rolled. James leaned over from the upper deck and fired on Jax at the same time. Jax ducked back for cover into a breezeway, throwing his back to the wall as bullets rained from above. The wall's arm slid a tactical knife across his throat, practically severing his head from body. Don, covered in his brother's blood, with the look of an enraged bull mastiff on his face, shoved Jax's body back through the doorway and watched the bullets riddle his corpse.

James stopped firing and moved on as Don peeked around the corner, catching a glimpse of Chris heading down the stairwell to the main deck. She hadn't cleared her section or announced her deviation. This was going against their plan of action and rubbed Don the wrong way, so he followed, announcing that the level had been cleared.

*****

Woody and the Proctor were stuck for the moment. Patty and Ray were at a vantage point, containing them to the rear stairwell. The only other way up was the elevators, so they held out, returning fire when they could.

"Rear stairwell, between one and two," Woody called.

"Pinned down, two, maybe three guns. Copy?"

"En route, couple of mics," James responded, working his way down. "Ken? Check in."

"Main deck, not secure. I repeat. Main deck, not secure, had a little setback," I said. Bullets reverberated through the mic before I keyed out.

I exchanged fire, placing a few rounds into a chest, and reloaded just outside the state room. Something didn't feel right. The windows were clean compared to much of the yacht. Plus they were covered completely. No way to look in or out.

I turned, kicked the door at the strike and spun, placing my back against the wall on the other side, expecting bullets to fly. None came. I crouched a little lower than normal, centered and pivoted through the door with my gun drawn. My heart dropped as I took in the scene before me.

There was no doubt in my mind that the two girls to my left were dead. Mutilated beyond recognition with sheer pain contorted on their faces. To my right was Lucy, battered and barely conscious.

"Ken?" she whispered as if reality was uncertain.

I collapsed on the floor in her lap and held back my tears. My emotions were playing against each other. But the most important thing was that Lucy was alive.

"We're getting out of here, baby. Hang in there."

I rushed out of the room and back to the last guy I had killed. "Cuff key, cuff key, cuff key," I said as I rummaged through his pockets frantically.

*****

Starboard of the main deck, Chris fired upon Dillon as he ducked into the bar. She slowed and crouched down at the filthobscured glass, held her position and cleaned off a small spot to peer through. No movement, no Dillon. She stayed down and scooted along the framing beneath the window towards the slider.

Chris tried to control her breathing and steady herself. Too much was at stake to chicken out now. Maxwell had to die and this was her opportunity.

Just before she made her move the pane above her shattered, blasting bullets and glass inches from her head. Dillon's country-strong arms followed the fragments as he reached through over the framing and grabbed Chris like a sack of dog food. He launched her into the bar room, pulling her gun free as her body impacted the floor.

"What do we have here? If it isn't Portman's little pet," Dillon snarled. "I knew he was behind this."

"The money's not there, Dillon," Chris blurted to stop the beast in its tracks.

Dillon kicked her hard in the ribs and put his boot on her skinny hip, shoving her to her back. "What money?"

"The wire transfers. Patrick set up the wire to bounce back, reversing the funds to Alex's accounts after you verified. You didn't really think he was going to just hand over $1.2 billion to an unstable fuck like you…"

Her head hit the floor before she could finish the sentence. Dillon pulled the shotgun back. "You're lying. Patty's been with me for twenty years," he shouted, beginning to lose control.

Chris blinked a few times, clearing the stars. "Brings new light to the term 'inside man,' doesn't it?"

"How did you find me?"

"It wasn't that hard. You're a total idiot. We knew you would take that girl. How do you say -- creature of habit?"

"Lucy?" Dillon said, contemplating for a moment. "From the fights… that's right, that's where I first saw her. Portman's idea or yours?"

"Do you know her man? He's got more drive and money than he knows what to do with and he's head over heels for her. We knew he would do whatever it took to hunt you down."

"Yeah, I think we've met," Dillon said, cringing at the memory.

"This was the only way we could get the launcher, Dillon… it was strictly business."

Don had heard enough. He threw his shoulder around the vacant windowpane and put a nine millimeter slug into Dillon's back. Dillon dropped to his knees as Chris quickly pulled the handgun she had been eyeing from his leg holster and pumped a round into his forehead. His body blew back as Chris stood over him and put another round through his left eye like a trained assassin.

Chris took a deep breath and looked over at Don, noticing the blood. "Thank you," she said softy.

Don responded with a look of utter disgust, raised the nine, sighted the weapon and pulled the trigger. The back of Chris' head exploded like a morning glory on the 4th of July. Don turned and paused for the sound of her body connecting with the floor. Temporarily satisfied, he returned to the mission at hand without looking back.

*****

James knew exactly where Woody and the Proctor were, but couldn't get a shot off or close enough to sling a grenade. He thought if he could get just inside the wall from their aggressors, he could leave a little present of C-4 and send them out to sea. He passed over their position, looked out over the railing from directly above the gunfire and raised a brow in thought. He quickly unraveled the survival cord from his wrist and tied one end around a grenade. After measuring out ten feet of cord he gripped the spoon, pulled the pin, tossed over the edge and timed the tension. The grenade flung back onto the decking at the feet of Ray and

Patty, catching them both off guard. Before they could form a thought, the explosion flashed, sending shrapnel in all directions. Ray was launched over the rail to the salt water and Patty went flying down the stairs to the bullets of Woody and the Proctor.

*****

I was releasing Lucy from the restraints as Don came in and stopped cold in his tracks.

"Oh God, Ken," he said. "Is she alive?"

"Yes, grab that wheelchair," I said, pointing across the room.

The scene made Don as sick as I was. We couldn't imagine what these girls went through or what had been done to Lucy.

Don brought the chair over and assisted me. Lucy was slightly coherent but otherwise dead weight.

"Where's John?" I asked.

Don looked me in the eyes and shook his head. Tears glossed as he spoke, "Let's just get Lucy loaded, Ken. I'll grab John while you secure the rest of the crew. Oh yeah, Chris won't be coming with us. I'll explain in the air."

*****

We were all loaded and ready to go when Don pushed his brother towards us in an old laundry cart. John's body was covered with bloody linens and would need to be wrapped properly for the trip home. The blood-soaked cotton weighted us all with hopeless despair. James and Woody took control of the situation, taking the cart from Don with a nod.

We sat in silence with our heads hung, waiting for John's body to be loaded. I squeezed Lucy's hand while mixed emotions threatened me. *I love you, Lucy.*

Woody gave the thumbs up for liftoff. Not a word was spoken until after The Claiborne was submerged with all its blood and crew. The explosion was a sight to see but enjoyed by none. My heartstrings -- along with the crew's -- were being pulled in all directions. Bittersweet could not even describe the emotions we were all experiencing as the fireball dissipated and The Claiborne sank in our rear view.

Don drummed up the strength to tell of Alex and Chris, driving our frustration and anger to a new level.

"So by eliminating Dillon, Alex Portman gets one hundred percent of the EL40," I said, looking down at the floor of Portman's hovercraft. "That means all of this was over a weapon?"

"In a nutshell," Don said.

*And Lucy was bait.*

*****

We returned to Stella's and got Lucy to Shafter's premier medical facility. Don returned to California to make arrangements for John's body, while James and I stayed with Lucy. The rest of the crew returned to Pensacola richer by one large hovercraft, compliments of Portman Industries.

## Chapter Twenty

The smell was sterile; sounds of monitors, beeps and hums filled the silence. Tubes ran from Lucy -- EKG wires and IV -- still beautiful through the trauma. Lucy physically bounced right back thanks to Shafter's state-of-the-art medical facility and professional staff. But her brain was stuck in purgatory. It was as if Dillon's memories lived on; lurking in the dark, back street shadows of Lucy's neural pathways.

Lucy had been waking up in panicked sweats throughout the nights. Sometimes she could recall the images in her dreams and other times just the emotional stresses were left to linger. No one could imagine what she had been through or laid witness to.

"Have you talked to Don?" James asked as he returned to Shafter's recovery unit with fresh fish tacos to please our palates.

"Funeral's next Monday, Pacific Burial did the cremation. Service is at ten at their Mission Mortuary," I said.

James just shook his head as he separated the tacos.

"Has she been out the whole time?" he asked, pointing to Lucy with his eyes.

"Yeah, she keeps twitching though."

Lucy bolted upright. "Stop! Stop! Stop!" she yelled as she pulled at the IV in her arm.

I pushed her back down. James dropped the tacos to help. Lucy was strong as a man, abnormally strong. It took everything we had to keep her from hurting herself or us. She thrashed and convulsed, mumbling incoherently for what seemed like minutes. Slowly her body calmed back to a relaxed state and we released our grasp.

James looked at me with that fathering worried expression.

"We're going back to that Neuralink facility as soon as she gets cleared," I said. "This is ridiculous. I don't know what is in her head. And half the time she can't even talk about it."

"Sounds like our only option, Ken. Maybe we should leave now, just take her, she's good to travel. You are the only thing that's going to free her from this nightmare."

I knew we would have to leave soon if we wanted a chance to link, recover and make the funeral on Monday. But I needed fuel and rest as much as Lucy. I ate my tacos and laid with Lucy for a bit while James made some phone calls and did a little research on Neuralink.

*****

A few hours' rest and I awoke. My body rhythm must have helped to calm Lucy. She slept solid as long as she was in my arms.

"I've got an address, Brian Frazier," James said when he noticed me stir. "He's one of the original co-founders of Neuralink. Still works out of the same facility where that Snyder guy you told me about did your original procedure."

"Well, let's go pay Mr. Frazier a visit," I said with a scratch in my voice.

I explained to the nurse that we would be departing and for her to prep Lucy for the trip as best as possible. Getting a scoff as a response, she did as I asked and Lucy was signed out and ready to go within the hour. The doctor hovered as I returned the pen to the overweight receptionist. He apparently felt the need to reiterate his disapproval. I held his gaze, thanked him for the professional job that he and his staff had provided, shook his hand and nodded farewell.

*****

The address led us to a breathtaking ranch home on twenty acres of rolling grass and cacti amidst a red rock gorge with a background panoramic view of the famous Camelback Mountain.

The home was draped with rust colored clapboard siding, a full wraparound porch, red steel roofing -- six and twelve pitch -- trimmed with patina copper downspouts and gutter.

There wasn't as much haze in the country so we had a clear view as we approached the plantation.

"What's the plan?" James asked as we circled once more.

"We ring the doorbell. Doesn't look like this guy has a worry in the world," I said. "No fence, no security."

"Maybe he is a badass with a samurai sword. Or possibly booby traps? Ring the bell; catch a blow dart to the throat. That kind of thing."

"It's time, old man. Let's introduce ourselves."

We touched down in plain sight and were greeted by two Bluetick Coonhounds.

I looked at James, "Okay, maybe he's good with a shotgun."

The dogs did their job intimidating. With their heads held high, tails rigid, showing no sign of fear or nervousness, they vocally announced their presence and ours.

"Can I help you boys?" a man said from a porch swing, making no effort to put his cold beer down.

"Mr. Frazier? We're looking for a Brian Frazier," I shouted over the dogs.

He whistled loudly and yelled, "Heal." The dogs quickly responded to the porch and assumed their positions. "Well, it's your lucky day… in the present."

He was an older man with white hair and an early slave owner disposition. Definitely not the scientist type I was expecting. *Maybe he was the money man*, I thought.

Mr. Frazier rose as we approached the steps, set his beer down and leaned casually against the turn post. We gave a formal introduction and shook hands, keeping one eye on the dogs. His hospitality was very southern. This man was not only on the wrong side of the country, he was also clearly born in the wrong era.

"Why don't you bring that young lady into the house," Mr. Frazier said, gesturing towards the hovercraft. "My wife can give her some lemonade."

We were not quite sure how he knew we had a third to our party but nevertheless we were impressed.

"We're kind of in a hurry, Mr. Frazier. We are in need of your services," I said, trying to match his politeness.

"Nonsense, bring her in and we'll talk," he said exposing a slight stubbornness.

I turned and saw Lucy peeking her head out of the craft and waved her in. I met her halfway and took her arm over my shoulder, helping her up the stairs. Frazier held the door and Lucy gave a thankful smile to our host in passing.

We stepped down into a cozy sunken living room. Not a thing modern tainted this beautiful home.

"I know, I know, lemonade. Come on, hon," Miss Frazier said to Lucy without introducing herself and took her to the kitchen. It was like she was grandma and everyone knew it. It was clear Lucy would be in good, caring hands.

After we explained our dilemma Mr. Frazier remained silent, thinking, as if he was solving mathematical proofs in his head.

"Snyder. Self-righteous prick, I must say. I'm glad he's gone. He was bad news from day one. My colleagues and I were in fact pushing him out; it's just easier said than done. Snyder went rogue morally, I guess is the way to put it. And what wrongs he has caused can never be corrected. I apologize deeply for his actions. I can, in fact, reconnect you with the Neuralink procedure. But you must understand... the damage has been done."

"If she relinks with Ken won't that free her mind from Dillon?" James asked.

"It doesn't quite work that way. In a perfect world, maybe. Memories are burned into our brains like a flesh wound. You can heal from bad memories but really they are just being masked with scar tissue."

"I think I understand," I said.

"It needs to be out in the open before we proceed, Ken," he said. "No false expectations. When you align your neural pathways you are merging past thoughts. Memories will mesh together as one. Any of the memories which he willed her to have will join with her own and become almost indistinguishable. Now when you link back, some of Dillon's thoughts could surface in both of you.

In essence, you would share in her burden."

"I thank you for your honesty, Dr. Frazier, but this must be done and we don't have a lot of time. I need to help Lucy through this and our presence is needed in California tomorrow afternoon," I said. "So if I may be curt, clock's ticking."

"I understand, Ken. Let me make some calls and then we can head over to the surgery center. I would be glad to help, seeing as you did us all a huge favor."

I nodded my head in thought as he made his exit. *What will it be like to have a killer in my brain? Will it change me? Lucy did things she never would have imagined she could. Will I?*

Grandma and Lucy brought out some lemonade on a serving tray. We quenched our thirst as Lucy relaxed on the plush sofa. She already looked stronger and more at ease. But I knew the battle was far from over.

We left shortly after and followed Dr. Frazier to his clinic where we met some of his on-call staff who were already preparing for the emergency procedure. Professional and well-briefed, they went to work setting us up. *Deja vu.*

*****

The funeral was beautiful beyond words. People from all over attended. James and Janet stood arm and arm to one side with Lucy. Lucy was radiant. Miller showed with Woody and, of course, the Proctor in tow. They too stood off to the side. Don and I were standing in the front facing the crowd during John's favorite Johnny Cash tune while friends and family packed the church-like pews before us. As I looked at the standing crew I realized that we shared something special. Very special. The music stopped and it was my turn. Lucy smiled at me, warming my heart.

I took a deep breath. "The calm before the storm," I said, adjusting the height of the microphone. "My name is Ken Detrick. I am a close friend of the family. This is my first experience with a eulogy and I am extremely honored, though I didn't have much time to prepare. So please bear with me. A few of you are familiar with the circumstances leading up to today. If you are not, rest assured, John died saving lives. Lives that are very dear to us all." I made eye contact with Lucy, then glanced to my left at Don. "But those lives we can celebrate tangibly. Today we celebrate the life of John Parker.

"I've known John for over twenty years. He was a handful in life and will undoubtedly be a handful in death. Look out, heaven," I said, glancing up to the ceiling, pulling a few chuckles.

"Fearless and impulsive describes his nature best. His brother Don was always the rational one though. I can recall some of Don's words as a youth. 'Don't double dog dare him, Ken. Don't do it, please,' he would say, shaking his head. Because he knew John would do it.

"John died way too young. I always thought he would be here. Right here. Old men smoking cigars and reminiscing about the good times… But John lives on within all of his friends and family. Not a day will pass that he will not be thought of.

"He was a generous man who lived life to the fullest. His only adversary in this world was boredom. John was a firm believer that being bored was a direct reflection of your own personality. And those of you that spent more than an hour with John can attest that he was in constant search of a good time. If it was out there, he would find it.

"Many of you might not know this, but Don and John were actually born in Canada. They spent most of their youth salvaging crab pots and fishing debris after storms off the coast of Victoria. John loved the open waters, the wind, bad weather and most of all, strong currents that challenged the hunt.

"And I know this for a fact, people. He looked up to his brother Don," I said in a whisper, like I was telling a dirty joke in Sunday school. "Though he would never admit it... his actions spoke it.

"John's passing was the ultimate sacrifice. Nothing shy of a soldier's death. A hero's death. And he is to be honored as such. "Today at the spreading of his ashes over the beautiful Pacific Ocean, we will perform our own version of a 21-gun salute; 10-gauge style. I hope you all can join us in honoring John's life and sacrifice.

"But let me tell you one last thing before I turn the floor over to young Rocky. I'm going to share the image of John that has been forever burned into my brain. It was early morning far out in Alaskan waters. I was up after a short night of rough see-sawing sleep and heard a screeching war cry. Flashing in my peripheral was John, buck naked, running for the bow. I knew better, but looked up, catching sight of John's pink bare moon launching into a swan dive over the railing. Keep in mind it's like twenty below and God knows how cold the water was. Don was laughing uncontrollably at my side. He looked at me and said..." I looked at Don to finish the line.

"He lost at poker again, grab the net," Don said, laughing through his tears.

# Chapter Twenty-One

"I love it," Lucy said as she straddled my lap.

I looked out over the ocean as she snapped photos of the pier.

"It's the same camera, Lucy," I said. She put it in my face.

"No, it's not. This one has special powers. I can look deep into your heart with this one," she said, smiling as she focused in on my cornea.

"Oh yeah? What do you see?"

"I see that you're happy, Ken Detrick. You're happy that your father agreed to move out here -- with a little persuasion from Janet, of course."

She moved the camera and placed her forehead to mine.

"That is true, I am happy. What else do you see?" I asked.

"Look into my eye… Pick a number between one and ten."
"Three," I said and she kissed me with all her might.

"My thoughts exactly. Now let's take this to the bedroom and get started, my little Casanova."

*****

"Mr. Portman, your next appointment is ready," the secretary said to the intercom. She looked at Don, smiled with southern dimples and winked.

"Alaskan contract? Send him in," Portman replied.

Don rose to his feet, stomped his right Durango boot to drop the pant leg and headed for the hunter green office doors. Guss blocked his move and gestured for a pat-down.

"Again? Your other guys don't do a good enough job?" Don complained.

"You can never be too careful, Mr. Longaker," Guss stated, serious as a heart attack.

Don submitted once more to the cursory search and entered the room through the heavy doors.

"Mr. Longaker, long way from home. I'm Alex Portman," Alex said, rising and taking Don's hand for a proper greeting. Alex paused the motion mid-shake while maintaining his grip and cocked his head quizzically. "Have we met before, Mr. Longaker? You look very familiar."

"I don't believe so. I haven't been in your neck of the woods for some time now." Don's acting was worthy of an Oscar, his accent sealing the deal.

"One would believe you hail from Texas with a name like that," Alex said, releasing his grip.

He shifted around his cherry wood topped desk and took his seat as Don lowered to the edge of the spare.

"Originally, that would be correct. My family's in the oil business and when the gold dried up, well, you can do the math. But fishing is my game, Mr. Portman. And protection is paramount. Have you looked over my proposal?"

"That I have," Alex said, taking a slow glance out the window then returning his forearms to the edge of the desk. "And you have come to the right place."

"I'm sure I have come to the right place."

Alex glared at Don, lowering his brow slightly, trying to pin his familiarities and strange tone. "I'll tell you what," Alex said, picking the file up from the desktop blotter and placing it back in the desk drawer, closing firmly. "I'm going to take one more look-see at the counter before we continue this conversation. Let's do lunch tomorrow. I'll have my guy pick you up. Just leave your information with Kim on your way out."

Don had expected this response but had to play up the part a bit more and show some disdain. "I've come a long way, Mr.

Portman and I believe you have had adequate time to consider a counter."

Portman glared with steel in his eyes. "Like I said, Mr. Longaker, lunch tomorrow."

Don read the 'take it or leave it glare,' threw his hands on his knees and stood to move on. "She was one of your calendar girls last year, am I wrong?" he asked, gesturing to the lobby.

Portman reflected again… "That's right, cover girl, in the flesh. Ask for an autograph on your way out," he said, nodding towards the door.

"Will do… Have a good day, Alex," Don said speaking his first name with clear malice as he made his exit.

After some brief flirting with Kim at the reception desk, a real autograph and a fake address, Don leaned in with seductive body language, kissed her hand, winked and was gone.

"Mr. Portman?" Kim called. "I'll be back in ten. Maintenance is in the lobby," Kim said, locking eyes with the stone cold Guss who was back to his usual creepy glare.

"Kim, before you step out, send Guss in."

She raised her eyebrows. "No problem, Mr. Portman." She cocked her head sideways and shrugged her shoulders at the muscle.

Guss moved his giant frame through the doorway and took a seat across from Alex. "What's up, boss?"

"Did that… Mr. Longaker look familiar to you?" Alex asked.

"As a matter of fact he did."

They were both silent for a moment. Alex got up and lingered looking out the window again. "Well?"

"I just can't put my finger on it, boss, sorry."

"Something about him rubbed me wrong. Get the address when Kim comes back and take some guys over there. Find out who the fuck this…"

The office exploded, casting fragments of Portman, Guss and cherry wood at a thousand feet per second out over the Chicago River, superseded by a massive fireball as Don's glider accelerated through the labyrinth of buildings snaking through the city. Bright yellow and red colors filled the rear view monitor… *Mission accomplished.*

Kim's eyes stayed glued to the screen as she whispered in Don's ear, "Good riddance." She kissed his neck as they shot up beneath the jet stream, bound for beautiful… sunny… California.